D0114635

THE GOAT

The Goat

ANNE FLEMING

Groundwood Books
House of Anansi Press
Toronto Berkeley

Groundwood Books / House of Anansi Press
groundwoodbooks.com

We acknowledge for their financial support of our publishing program the Canada
Council for the Arts, the Ontario Arts Council and the Government of Canada.

 Canada Council   Conseil des Arts
for the Arts   du Canada

 ONTARIO ARTS COUNCIL
CONSEIL DES ARTS DE L'ONTARIO
an Ontario government agency
un organisme du gouvernement de l'Ontario

With the participation of the Government of Canada   Canadä
Avec la participation du gouvernement du Canada

Library and Archives Canada Cataloguing in Publication
Fleming, Anne, author
The goat / Anne Fleming.
Issued in print and electronic formats.
ISBN 978-1-55498-916-4 (hardback).—ISBN 978-1-55498-917-1
(epub).—ISBN 978-1-55498-918-8 (mobi)
I. Title.
PS8561.L44G62 2017   jC813'.54   C2016-905754-2
C2016-905755-0

Jacket art by Josie Portillo
Jacket design by Michael Solomon

Printed and bound in Canada

MIX
Paper from
responsible sources
FSC
www.fsc.org   FSC® C016245

For Kate

1

Once there was a mountain goat who lived in New York City. The building he lived on had great views and many sturdy ledges to stand on high above the metropolis.

Unfortunately, not much grew on the building. Not much a goat could eat.

True, there was that bucket of hay that appeared on the upper ledge each morning. And there were cedars on the penthouse deck, and people put out window boxes every now and then.

But the bucket was a snack, he'd eaten the cedars down to the bark, and geraniums don't go far when you're a goat.

One or two tenants persisted in planting and re-planting, determined to have success with one hardy breed of plant or another. But at last, even Mrs. Fenniford-Lysinski had to concede defeat.

For a while it seemed as if wheatgrass had done the trick. It grew faster than any plant Doris Fenniford-Lysinski had ever met. But Doris's wheatgrass never grew past two inches, and one day she discovered it chewed right down to the roots.

"How can grass un-grow?" Doris asked her husband, Jonathan.

"I o o," said Jonathan from behind the paper.

Doris kept a keen eye on her wheatgrass, but she never saw anything eating it. That's because the goat waited for Doris to go to the bathroom before he mowed the wheatgrass with his teeth.

"O," replied Jonathan, when Doris came back and asked how on earth her grass had un-grown while she was in the loo.

"O" meant "goat," but unfortunately Doris could not understand Jonathan because Jonathan had had a stroke that impaired his speech. Since he could not make Doris understand, Jonathan went back to the paper.

In truth, Jonathan liked knowing that the goat had eaten the wheatgrass and that Doris did not know. He could have written it down (as he was wont to do when he absolutely had to communicate with Doris), or rather typed it on the little tablet computer she had bought him, but he didn't feel like it.

Jonathan didn't feel like much, these days.

One morning, a kid named Kid moved into the building. Kid knew nothing about the goat. How could she? She was from Toronto.

"We're in New York!" Kid's mom said when their plane landed. "Where we're going to live! For a very short time! Because our show will close within a week!"

Actually, regardless what happened with the show, they were staying at least four months — maybe six — depending on the cousin.

The cousin was a distant one. Wealthy, older, prone to popping off to pleasant climes for four to six months at a time. Normally he took his dog with him. But this time he was going to England, where they didn't allow dogs.

"What?" Kid said. "They don't allow dogs in England?"

"Well, they do, obviously," said her dad. "Walkies and everything." Here he imitated a famous British dog trainer from before Kid was born. "But they quarantine them. If you want to move to England with a dog you have to leave it in a kennel for half a year."

So they were looking after the cousin's dog. While leaving Kid's cat at home with Nana. How was that fair?

They were also staying in the cousin's apartment. Near Central Park. Where they were pulling up right now.

Her mother was just about falling over with excitement.

"Look! It has an awning," cried Kid's mom.

Kid looked. Yes, a narrow green canvas canopy stretched from the door across the sidewalk to the curb. Woo.

"That's great, Lisa," Kid's dad said. "Can you pay the cab driver?" He got out of the cab. Kid roused herself enough to do the same.

It was early. They had got up at four in the morning to catch their flight. She was very sleepy.

"I'm paying a cab driver in New York!" Kid's mom said, then folded up her wallet and got out of the car.

A man with a maroon captain's hat and matching jacket with brass buttons opened the door under the awning.

"There's a doorman!" Lisa said in a stage whisper. "Doorman!" she said in a regular voice. "Hello!"

"Lady!" said the doorman as he intercepted the suitcases from Kid's dad. "Can you get the door?"

"I'm getting the door for the doorman!" said Lisa. "In New York!"

Kid was too tired to pay much attention, but as she rolled her eyes, she thought she saw a blur of white at the top of the building, like a tiny low-hanging cloud.

The tiny low-hanging cloud was the goat. The goat was hungry. Hungry, hungry, hungry.

Just over the way, just over *there*, was food. A valley full of it. Grass. Flowers. Leaves. Reeds. Bark. All kinds of stuff.

All he had to do was trip to the back of the foothill, zip down the clangy black cliff, drop to the ground, tuck around the corner, navigate the gray purposeless ledge — who needs a ledge on the ground? — and cross the black river of giant moving clumps.

He would go do it right now. Yes, he would. Yes, he *was* doing it. He was trotting along the ridge to the clangy cliff. He was looking down the clangy cliff, the only thing that lay between him and all the food he could eat …

Except for the gray purposeless ledge down in the valley. Oh, and the noisy tree-ish creatures that roamed the ledge. Plus the river of giant moving clumps.

If only he could brave the clangy cliff at last. The clangy cliff and the purposeless ledge and the river of clumps.

Could he?

Yes. He could. Definitely. Today. Right n —

— later. Right now he needed to eat.

He leapt a zig — *clang* — and a zag — *clang* — of the cliff. The clangs, it must be said, were the lightest of clangs. His hooves had soft inner pads that cushioned each landing. The noisy tree-ish creatures did not even seem to hear them.

But they were still clangs. The goat paused and danger-checked after each one.

He leapt to the bucket ledge. Paused. Danger-checked. Went on. Turned the corner.

There it was, the bucket. Full, said his nostrils. He trotted closer, danger-checked.

Was the cave-cover closed?

Yes. Yes, it was.

All right. It was safe. Safe-ish. Mm, the smell was so good. The taste so good. Eating was so good. So so good. So so …

Over. The bucket was empty.

Time to check the grass. The grass was back around the corner and one ledge down.

Had it grown back yet? Had it?

It had not.

Back up to the roof. Back along the ridge. Back to the cedars. Up on his hind hoofs.

Could he reach? He could not. He'd have to jump. Jump and bite. Jump and bite.

He spent the next hour jumping for cedar. With each jump he felt a tiny inner memory of gamboling, his early days with his mother on the cliffside.

One day he would gambol again. One day. When his stomach was full. When he was safe.

Safe-ish. You were never entirely safe.

Here came the soft-footed friendly wolfish thing.

Good morning. It feels good to pee, doesn't it?

The soft-footed friendly wolfish thing was a seeing-eye dog, a yellow lab named Michigan. Michigan went back inside through the doggie door off the penthouse deck and nosed his owner's hand.

"What's that noise, Michigan?" said his owner, Joff. "That hoofy noise. Like the pigeons are wearing wooden shoes. Felted wooden shoes."

Michigan wagged his tail. Michigan knew it was a goat. Michigan and the goat were friends. But Michigan had no way of telling Joff that.

"I'm not getting very far, Michigan," said Joff.

He was working on a novel that was going to be totally different from the last book. No dragons. No samurai. *The Plates of Barifna*, it was called. Joff worked every night from one in the morning until seven or until he had written two thousand words, whichever came first.

Right now it was 6:55.

He had written thirty-six words.

The plates of Barifna were not dinner plates but tectonic plates. Barifna was a planet whose core was heating up and so its tectonic plates were moving at a much faster rate than they do on earth and smashing mountains into place within a month or two. Volcanoes erupted continuously along subversion zones.

Barifna had been a happy planet until exploited by human-like people, who treated it like one vast mine, extracting ore that they needed to fuel their warp-speed inter-planetary travel. Now it was taking revenge. The people did not realize that Barifna was a sentient planet in a galaxy of sentient planets, but by the end of the book they would. They would learn that they were, in fact, parasites, and that it is not in the interest of parasites to kill their host.

His main character, Martin —

What was that noise?

Joff went out to the deck, Michigan by his side. The air misted his cheeks.

Was that a snort?

"Who's there?" he said, not really thinking anyone was. But something *had* made a clop noise. Something *had* made a snorty sound.

Was that breathing he heard beyond his own and Michigan's? He could not say.

He heard pigeons *prr*ing, shouts from the street

twelve stories below. The clanging of truck doors going up. The wheels of hand-trucks rolling.

"Spiderman in clogs? Clogman? Superman with a cold and lead feet?"

He rubbed a hand over his face, feeling the stubble on his jaw.

"Maybe I just need to sleep."

His computer beeped at him. Seven o'clock. He groaned.

"All right," he said. "I'm going to sleep. I'm going to sleep, and tonight, I'll nail it. I'll sit down, type-type-type-type-type, and two thousand words will appear just like magic. I'll nail it."

He brushed his teeth, washed his face, put in his earplugs, fell into bed and then fell into sleep.

Three floors down, in Apartment 908, Jonathan was waking up. He opened his left eye. His right stayed half-shut.

Another day. Grump. Doris was in the bathroom, singing. She had the coffee on. He could smell it. She'd be in in a moment.

Good morning, she'd say cheerfully, whipping off the covers like a peppy, mad nurse. *Let's get these limbs moving!*

Here she was now. Her white hair was neatly brushed, her neck scarf neatly knotted. Good God, she looked like an airline stewardess!

"Good morning!" she said cheerfully. She whipped off the covers. "Let's get these limbs moving!"

Jonathan groaned. She lifted his right leg and manipulated it so his knee bent then straightened, bent and straightened, bent and straightened.

"Now you," she shouted.

I can hear you, he fumed in his head.

He lifted his leg about two inches off the bed, then dropped it.

"Again. Left leg. Come on, now," shouted Doris.

Lift. Drop. Bah.

"Arm," shouted Doris. "Come on, Jonathan."

Leave me alone.

She wrangled his arm, not reading his telepathy at all, or ignoring it if she did.

"Now, up you get." Doris helped Jonathan into a sitting position. She brought his walker forward, helped him stand, helped him get on his housecoat, let him fumble his way into the bathroom.

At least she let him pee alone now. Jonathan finished, washed and grumbled and shuffled to the breakfast table.

"Lift your feet, darling," said Doris. "Do try."

Jonathan glowered.

"I've got wonderful hot cereal for you."

And so it went. Unrelenting cheerfulness. Minimal movement from maximum effort. Troops of people in and out of the house to "help him get better." Physiotherapist, occupational therapist, massage therapist, speech therapist. All madly cheerful, all career optimists.

And he could do nothing about it, not even tell Doris to shut up.

"What flavor wheatgrass juice would you like this morning? Banana-strawberry? Kiwi-lime? Blueberry?"

Vinegar vomit, thought Jonathan.

"I know you don't like it, dear, but it does do wonders! All that chlorophyll!"

I am not a plant. You've been duped by yet another fad.

After delivering his vinegar vomit, Doris brought the wheatgrass in again.

"It's not pigeons eating it," she said. "What else could it be? You don't get rats up this high, do you?"

Jonathan didn't answer.

"Jonathan, I wish you'd talk to me," said Doris.

"I a," he shouted.

"Don't be silly," she said. "Of course you can."

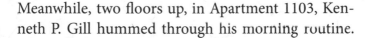

Meanwhile, two floors up, in Apartment 1103, Kenneth P. Gill hummed through his morning routine.

He brought in the empty hay bucket from the ledge, leaving the window open, just in case. He showered, shaved, put on his nicely ironed shirt and his pleasing suit, his spiffy shoes. He phoned his mom, sent an email to his ex-wife, arranged dinner with friends and tried not to think too much about the goat.

Goat? he said to himself. What goat?

2

Down in the lobby, a tall man with a big-headed white dog at his knee held out both hands toward Kid's dad.

"Bobby!" he cried, putting his hands on Kid's dad's cheeks just as if he were ten. "Look at you, all grown up. I haven't seen you since you were this kid's age!"

He tossed Kid's dad's head back and forth between his two hands. "Hello! Welcome!"

"I'm Doug," he said to Kid and her mom. Kid feigned extra sleepiness in order to look like she was not paralyzed by shyness. He looked down at the dog. "This is Cat."

Cat? Kid was leaving her actual, real cat at home to look after a dog with a big nose and weeny eyes named *Cat*?

Cat wagged her tail.

"This is Lisa," said Kid's dad. "And Kid."

Doug shook Kid's hand. His was big and warm and like his face smiling down on her it radiated bonhomie.

But she could only get her eyes as far as his ear. That was what happened when she met new people.

"Doug and Cat?" said Kid's mom, raising her eyebrows.

"Kid?" said Doug with the same expression.

There was a pause and then both moved their shoulders in a way that meant, *I like you.*

"What a relief," said Doug in the elevator. "I *thought* you'd be the same, Bobby, but of course you never know. I couldn't leave Cat with just anybody."

The elevator doors opened.

"Properly, her name is Catherine the Great, but we've always called her Cat, haven't we?" Doug said, rubbing Cat's jowls. "Yes, we have."

Kid kept an eye out for someone else to explain the "we" business, but in the apartment there was a very small kitchen, a living room with a dining ell, one small bedroom and one tiny bedroom with a desk and a Murphy bed and no other people.

"Cat, of course, is the best dog in the world," he went on. "But you will discover that for yourselves. I'm leaving you *The Book of Cat.*" He showed them a hardcover book he had put together and went on to explain its contents. What food she liked, when she liked it, where she ate it, where she liked to go in the park, and so on.

Kid collapsed onto the couch. Cat jumped up, turned around twice, curled up next to her and put her chin on Kid's leg.

All right. Maybe she was sweet. But she was *not* the best dog in the world. The best dog in the world was a cat.

Wait. That was almost what Doug had said. Ha. Joke.

Kid fell asleep.

She slept until two in the afternoon and woke hungry. Someone had put a blanket over her.

Where was she?

Oh. New York. With Cat. The dog. Who was so warm. Mm. You could see her skin under her fur. On a lot of creatures this would be gross. On Cat it wasn't. It was perfect. Her eyes also seemed to convey perfect understanding. As if they were saying, *I am sorry you couldn't bring your cat.*

Kid found she had already forgiven her. Kid was simply not going to think about Fleabag. She was not.

There.

Faint noises arose from the street — car horns, engines, a bash and clang or two, the hissing of tires on wet roads. Closer, rain went *plat, plat* on the windows. The apartment itself was quiet.

Her parents must be sleeping, too. Yes, there was a little snort from her father, a sigh from her mother. She padded eight steps down the short hall and peered into the small bedroom. They lay in their clothes on the bed, her dad on his back, mouth open, her mother curled on her side.

Kid sighed. They were so excited about New York. They kept trying to explain what made it so much better than Toronto.

She wasn't convinced.

Here she was, though, in this neat, crowded living room with its tall dark bookshelves, comfy chairs, end tables neatly stacked with art books, and a dog on the couch.

It was okay but it was Someone Else's. It smelled different. Like pencils.

Two windows looked across a broad busy street to Central Park, gray and misty in the September rain, the treetops dulled to silver.

On the dining-room table was Doug's *The Book of Cat*. It was a sketchbook, really, with an ink-and-watercolor drawing on the front of Cat curled up on the couch, exactly as she was curled right now.

Doug was a good artist. Kid opened it.

Underneath another sketch of Cat, this time standing bulldoggishly with head cocked, it said, *My name is Catherine the Great. But you may call me Cat.*

Do you know the important things in life?

Each of the important things was illustrated.

Food. Here there was a food bowl.

Sleep. Cat asleep in three different poses.

Walks. Cat and Doug from behind on a path in the woods.

Rats. An overhead view of a rat running away from Cat.

Singing. Cat and Doug singing.

Singing?

People. Three people sitting on a park bench, Cat running up to them.

Things that approximate rats. A tennis ball.

Here is how I like to spend my day:

It is extremely urgent that I get up and get everyone in the household up niiiice and early so we can go out and chase rats. Rat substitutes will do. Then we can come home and sleep. You may think that given how much I sleep after coming home, it would work just as well to sleep that sleep before going out. It would not. It's important to be vibrantly awake for short periods of time. It makes sleeping much much better. Later in the day, another walk is nice.

This is my blanket.

These are my friends. This was on a two-page spread, maybe a dozen little circles containing scenes of Cat's friends.

Cat had more friends than Kid did.

These are places that I like to go. With this was a map that made Kid want to go exploring. Any place was better when there was a map.

Her dad came out of the bedroom stretching and yawning.

"Here's looking at you, Kid," he said as usual.

"No, here's looking at you," said Kid.

"No, here's looking at *you*."

"*You.*" In former days, this exchange had ended in tickles, and in fact still sometimes did.

Today, though, her dad just stretched and gestured at the apartment.

"Pretty nice, eh?"

"It's all right."

Her dad imitated her. "'It's all right.' Come on. It's fantastic!"

"Kind of small."

"This is huge for Manhattan."

"Doug gone?"

"Doug's gone. How do you like Cat?"

"I like Cat." That was something she could say wholeheartedly. There was no point bringing up Fleabag again.

Cat, at the sound of her name, cocked her head back and forth, listening.

"Mom's play's going to be great, isn't it?"

"You know it."

Cat put her head back down.

"How come she's all *Augh! It's going to close in two weeks*?"

"Superstition. She's afraid of jinxing it. But also, it's a big deal opening a play in New York. A huge deal. I mean, huge."

"Do you ever wish you were in it?"

"No. I don't miss that life."

"But you're going to work on a play."

"I was never quite comfortable acting. I mean, nobody is. But some people *like* that kind of feeling uncomfortable. They feel it in their body. A zing. Like they're more alive. I never felt that. And somebody needed to pay the bills. And I like teaching math."

"You always say you hate it."

"Math itself is beautiful. It's high-school students that are the problem. Even they're not that bad. But when I started teaching, I always told myself I'd go back and finish that play I was working on and now I am."

"What's the play about?"

"It's … uh … well, it's about … uh … two friends. Sort of. Or brothers. And their families. And an accident. I don't really want to talk about it."

"He doesn't know what it's about," said Kid's mom matter-of-factly, emerging from the bedroom, pulling her hair back behind her neck.

"I know exactly what it's about. I just don't want to talk about it."

"Oh, hey, Mom."

"Here's looking at you, Kid."

"No, here's looking at *you*."

"Let's go for a walk in the park." Lisa paused for effect. "It'll be a walk in the park!"

Kid shook her head. Her parents. Sheesh.

By the time they'd unpacked enough to find their raincoats, it had stopped raining.

In the lobby, there was a different doorman in the same uniform.

"Doug told me about you," he said to them. "Welcome to New York. I'm Julio."

"Bobby," Kid's dad said. "I mean, Bob."

"Lisa," said Kid's mom.

Kid looked at Julio's shoulder. Once again, her eyes would go no farther. Her heart beat fast. *Flight!* it said.

"And this is Kid."

Kid opened her mouth in the shape of "Hi," but no sound came out.

The elevator dinged. An older woman dressed in a stylish skirt suit came out and went gaga over Cat. She was not the kind you'd think would go all silly with a dog, but there she was, wagging her butt and tapping Cat on the nose and scratching her chin.

"Who's an adorable ugly betty?"

There was another round of introductions. Kid looked at another shoulder. This one had shoulder pads and gold buttons.

The elevator dinged again. Out came a young man holding the harness of a seeing-eye dog in one hand and a skateboard in the other.

"Look, Cat, it's Michigan," said the stylish lady. Cat wagged her tail. Michigan wagged his tail.

"Hi, Mrs. Grbzc," said the guy with the skateboard.

"Good afternoon, Mr. Vanderlinden," said Mrs. Grbzc.

"Hi, Doug," he said next.

"It's not Doug," Bobby said. "It's — "

But skateboard guy was already through the lobby and out the door that Julio was holding open.

"Thanks, Julio." The guy turned right, dropped his skateboard, hopped on it and boarded off, Michigan keeping pace by his side.

"Um," said Kid's mom. "Was that just a blind skate-boarder?"

"That was not just any blind skateboarder," said Mrs. Grbzc. "That was Joff Vanderlinden."

When Joff's feet were on a skateboard, it was like riding a magic carpet. It was like the whole history of man and wheel. It was a way of knowing the pavement. He felt it in his foot muscles, his calf muscles, his toes, all the way up his legs. He rode with his knees bent, always at the ready for a cue from Michigan to cut left or right, to slow down for old people. Being on a skateboard reminded him that his whole body was alive, loose, ready, capable. His heart rate rose and flew like a bird.

Joff had been a boy wonder twice over. First he'd been the skateboarding blind kid boy wonder. It had started in his parents' rec room in upstate Michigan when he was a toddler and sat on his sister's skateboard as if it were a pushbike.

Later, he stood on it. He taught himself flip turns. His sister leaned couch cushions against the walls so he wouldn't hurt himself. When they got older, his sister took him to the schoolyard, where he went back and forth on the pavement. It was amazing to be able to go so far before he had to turn around. It was amazing to really carve turns.

They started building small jumps. It became a neighborhood thing, helping the blind kid skateboard. The local news caught wind of it and for a little while, he was famous. There were still videos on YouTube.

Next he was a teenage fantasy writer boy wonder. He had written a blockbuster book that if he was honest was really a knockoff of all the books he'd ever read. But he was proud of his grumpy little genie and gentle self-sacrificing kid nonetheless, not to mention the evil snake people who threatened to topple the powers of good. He sent it to an agent, who sent it to a publisher, who published it. People liked the book. It sold. He wrote another one. And another.

He figured he was really just lucky. Even if he had already started and abandoned eight untitled novels in the past two years. Even if the rent on his penthouse was gobbling up a greater and greater percentage of his income.

Skateboarding was the antidote to everything. He loved the feeling of movement under his feet, the unsteadiness, the need to be ready to react, the *roll-roll-roll-snick* of sidewalk cracks, the cries of people jumping out of his way, cursing at him, the sound of Michigan's nails on the sidewalk, the subtle pressure to and from the dog that communicated *left, right, slow down, stop, let's go!*

But chess. He was not a boy wonder at chess. He just liked it a whole lot.

You could tell you were at Washington Square Park not just because it was what you hit at the end of Fifth Avenue but because it sounded different and smelled different. No traffic noise bouncing off buildings and exhaust but birds singing, people shouting, a jazz trio playing, kids' feet on pavement, the crowing banter of the chess players, the *smock* of the play clock as turns changed, the smell of dying grass, cigarette smoke, popcorn and onions and hotdogs from the vendors.

Joff rolled up to the chess tables, stopped and flipped his board up into his hand.

"Yo, Joff," said Chili. "How's the mastodons?"

"Chili, keep up, man," said Ginger. "He's not writing that book anymore. The mastodons are history."

"Ginger, you're a comedian," said Mikael.

"It's faults, now. Right, Joff? The planet that takes tectonic revenge?"

"You got it, Ginge. Who's free for a game?"

He sat down with Chili and fell into the rhythm of play, felt his mind go calm. He lost two games, stalemated one, then stepped aside so Chili could play for money.

A kid asked Joff for a game and tried to cheat.

"Are you serious, kid? I got the game here," he said, pointing to his head. "You can't have made that move. Your knight wasn't there."

"Miles!" admonished his mother.

"Don't try to cheat the blind man, buddy," said Chili.

"All right, I'm sorry." The kid wanted to keep playing, but Joff had a personal rule.

"That's it, kid. Game over."

When he finally got rid of the kid, he was about ready to head off for a pee, a roti and a ginger beer, in that order, when someone new asked him for a game.

A female someone with a round voice. A voice like a well.

"Up for another game? My name's Mara."

"Mara? Joff."

"Joff?" said Mara.

"No, Joff."

"Aren't we saying the same thing?"

"I don't know. Are we?"

"I think so."

"Sorry. It's just that most people think I said Jeff.

And then I say, 'No, Joff,' and they say, 'Joff?' and I say, 'Joff,' and they say, 'What's that short for?'"

"And what do you say?"

"Nothing."

"Do you say the word, 'nothing'? Or do you sit there?"

"I say the word. Joff's not short for anything. It's Dutch. Should be 'Yoff,' really. I was born in Holland. My mom was born in Malaysia but moved to Holland when she was three."

"And who's the yella fella here?"

"That's Michigan."

"Funny name for a dog. Yes," her voice changed to a dog-patting voice, "that's a funny name for a dog." Back to regular voice. "Are we playing?"

"Sure."

"E4," Mara called her move and hit the play clock. *Smock.*

"What isn't a funny name for a dog?" asked Joff. "E5." *Smock.*

"I don't know. Whiskers. Nf3." *Smock.* "Mutt. Jeff. Joff."

"Nc6." *Smock.* "Whiskers is completely a — "

"Bb5." *Smock.* " — cat name."

"Barfy. Mr. Bone. A6." *Smock.*

Mara beat Joff the first game. And the second. And the third.

"Glad I never play for money," Joff said.

"You're making me wish I did," said Mara.

"Yeah? You do sometimes?"

"Oh, yeah. I'll totally lay down money with guys who think I'm going to be a pushover."

"How can you tell they think that?"

"Oh, you can tell. Trust me."

"Yeah, but how?"

"Different things. A grin. A tone. 'Put your money away, little lady. I don't wanna take your money.'"

"And what do you say?"

"Oh, you just try to take my money, buckaroo."

Later, on his way home, Joff realized he had a smile on his face. He'd been recalling different things Mara had said, and the way she said them.

The way she said "buckaroo" most of all.

Of course it was Joff Vanderlinden. Who else would the blind skateboarder be? Kid had read his dragon books. She had watched his skateboarding videos with her dad. And there he was ahead of them, standing on the corner, waiting for the light. There he was, coasting across the street. There he went, rolling down Central Park West.

Wow. Okay. Maybe New York was a tiny bit exciting.

The park smelled of mud and decayed leaves and fresh rain. Cat panted happily. Kid read Doug's map.

"This is one of the places where if you let her off the leash, Cat sometimes catches rats."

"Let's not let her off the leash," said Bobby.

Doug's notes told them there were surgical gloves inside the dog bag for picking up and disposing of the dead rats.

"I am not picking up dead rats," Bobby said.

"We're going to pick up rats! In New York City!" said Lisa.

Kid held Cat's leash. Lisa and Bobby held hands. They swung them back and forth. Every now and then, Lisa did a little happy hop.

"I can't believe we're here," she said. "I can't believe this is actually happening."

"You're in an Off-Broadway show," said Bobby, hip-checking her.

"I'm in an Off-Broadway show," Lisa repeated. She hopped again. "Who'd a thunk it?"

Kid's mom had dreamed of performing on or off Broadway since she was, in her words, a buck-toothed, stick-legged eight-year-old staging *Sweeney Todd* in her living room.

"I'd a thunk it," said Kid. Lisa had a great, surprising voice and perfect comic timing, but that wasn't the main thing. It was that you *believed* in her. Even her very own kid, sitting in the audience, started to believe she *was* the character she was playing. In this case, her character was not so far from her everyday self. She played an anxiety-prone feminist mom who worried soccer was teaching her son the wrong kind of competitiveness and aggression.

"Thanks, Kid. You're a sweetheart."

Lisa stuck out her free hand for Kid to hold so the three of them were hand in hand. And then the three of them began to skip.

Skipping was this amazing feedback loop. You skipped when you were happy, and even if you were being deliberately goofy, skipping only made you happier, so you wanted to skip more. When you finally stopped, you were almost always laughing.

Now they slid into the particular hop and skip that Dorothy, the Tin Man, Scarecrow and Cowardly Lion did as they sang that they were off to see the wizard. And then, of course, because they were doing the Wizard of Oz hop-skip, Kid and Bobby and Lisa had to sing.

"*Because, because, because, because, be-CAUSE,*" they belted.

And on that last note, they heard a funny sound.

Cat. Singing.

"A-roooo," she sang.

"*Because of the wonderful things he does.*"

People may have looked at them. It didn't matter. Kid was inside the family bubble.

They slipped back into an easy walk through the damp woods.

A little while later, an older woman jogged toward them.

"Hello, Cat," she said warmly to Cat.

And then she slowed, jogging in place, and directed a question at Kid.

"Where's Doug?" she asked.

Pop! The family bubble burst. Kid was hit with hot face, rigid gaze, rigid jaw, immobile tongue that came with a direct question from a stranger.

She wanted to answer. But words fled her mind. Her heart blocked her throat. *Flight!*

The woman turned and jogged backwards, waiting.

"England!" Lisa said for Kid. "England. Doug's in England."

The woman nodded, turned and ran on.

"Hey, I recognize her from the *Book of Cat*," said Bobby. "That's the grandmother who's run the New York Marathon every year for the last thirteen years."

"Can you take the leash?" said Kid to Lisa. "Please?"

"You can do it," Lisa said to Kid. "I know you can do it. You can answer when people ask you questions. Let's practice, okay? Where's Doug?"

"It's different with you," Kid said.

"I know," said Lisa. "But answers are readier on your tongue if you practice." She changed her voice to a gum-snapping New Yorker voice. "Where's Doug?"

"England," Kid grumbled.

Now her mom used her teenaged rapper voice. "Yo, where's Doug? Where's Doug-the-thug?"

"England," Kid said louder.

Her I've-smoked-for-sixty-years grandma voice. "Where's Doug?" She pretended to pick a piece of tobacco off her tongue as if from a hand-rolled cigarette.

"England!" Kid and Bobby shouted together.

"All right, people," said Smoky Grandma. "I think we've got ourselves a Kid who answers."

A little farther along the track, an older man with a rainbow yarmulke greeted Cat like Doug had greeted Bobby, with his hands out. He bent down and scratched Cat on the cheeks while she panted happily.

"Where's Doug?" he asked.

"England," all three of them said.

"Oh, it's the unison family," said the man. "Nice to meet you. Do you say everything in chorus?"

"No," they said in chorus.

"I don't believe you," he said in a sing-song voice, walking away now.

"Goodbye," they chorused.

They walked around the reservoir, which was basically a big lake, and along paths where the trees made a canopy over their heads. A small patch of blue appeared in the sky, shaped like a goose in flight.

"It does not get better than this," said Lisa.

Kid had to concede that maybe it was all right.

They wandered home through back streets lined with old buildings, tall ones and squat ones, blocky ones and narrow ones, ones with big steps like on *Sesame Street*. There were more awnings and doormen and lots of people — two ladies power-walking, a man with five little dogs on elastic leashes, a boy on a unicycle.

They turned a corner onto a street with stores. Lisa popped into a convenience store while Kid and Bobby stayed outside with Cat. She came out with a map in her hand.

"Here you go, Kid," she said.

A couple of blocks later there were four kinds of takeout.

"Jackpot!" said Lisa. "Your call, Kid. What do you want?"

Kid chose sushi.

Yet another doorman greeted them.

"Hello, Doug-replacements," he said. "What did you bring me for dinner?"

Kid gazed on yet another gold epauletted shoulder. Why were doormen even necessary? Everybody had keys, didn't they?

She felt grumpy again, and thirsty. As soon as they got into the apartment, she got herself a drink of water.

Doug's glasses all matched. They were square and heavy on the bottom and didn't feel right in her hand. At home she had a favorite glass. Small with blue-and-white stripes. How could you have favorites when all your glasses matched?

She took a drink. Pah. The water didn't taste right, either.

At least the sushi was good. But her parents wanted to go out again. There was a free concert at some gallery. They weren't tired after their sleep. They were in New York! Come on!

Kid sighed and grumbled but what choice did she have? She had to go to a stupid free concert.

She took a book, which turned out to be a wise choice. A woman played a vacuum-cleaner hose while a man shouted into a cardboard box.

On the way back, the subway was crowded. People jostled them and didn't say sorry. Somebody smelled really bad. Kid stuck her nose against her mother's coat sleeve.

Finally they made it home and Kid got to fold down the Murphy bed. She'd heard of them but never seen one. When it was up it was a bed-sized rectangle on the wall. You pushed it in a little, released a latch, and it lowered smoothly from the wall. When it was down, it took up three-quarters of the space, making the room nice and snug.

Kid's parents came in and gave her a good-night kiss and told her they loved her. When she was done reading and turned out the light, she took a deep breath and let it out slowly, ready for sleep to over-take her.

But it didn't. She lay awake missing the weight of Fleabag and thinking of her bedroom at home, the maps on the walls, her neat drawers. And her friends, asleep in their houses, and how funny it was that peo-ple lived all over the world and you never thought of them until you went someplace new.

Cat hopped up. Kid sighed.

"You're not as good as a real cat. You know that," Kid said.

Cat tucked her chin down as if to say, *You don't mean that*.

"Oh, all right," said Kid.

Cat turned in a circle three times and curled by Kid's side. In less than a minute, Kid was asleep.

•

Rehearsals for Lisa's show didn't start until Tuesday, so they had the weekend to do what they wanted. They walked Cat and gawked at the Statue of Liberty. Lisa cried at Ellis Island upon hearing the stories of im-migrants so much like her parents. They went to the Strand Bookstore and to Times Square, which was gaudy with advertisements and jammed with tour-ists like themselves, everybody with their phones in the air, taking pictures. Kid didn't see what the point was.

Back at the apartment, Lisa did vocal exercises in the bathroom while Cat sat outside the door and sang along.

Dear Luna, Kid wrote on her first postcard. *The Statue of Liberty looks huge from a boat in the harbor, but doesn't feel that big when you climb up inside. Dad's cousin calls him Bobby so now we are too. How was the second week of school? Your friend, Kid.*

The nearer time drew to Lisa's show starting rehearsals, the more Lisa fretted. On Tuesday itself, Lisa alternated between bouts of paralysis and spasms of frantic activity — assembling keys, lucky key ring, lucky socks, script, computer, Lucky Gumby figurine. Should she take an umbrella? It might rain. But if she took it, it might not rain, and then she would forget about it and lose it. Wasn't there something unlucky about lost umbrellas?

Kid and Bobby were going with her, if only to make sure she actually got to the rehearsal hall.

"Why did I say yes to this? What was I thinking?"

"Mom. It's going to be fine. It's going to be great."

"How can it be fine? I've sold out. I've totally sold out. 'Soccer Mom' is nothing like 'Hockey Mom.' Soccer, hockey, they're totally different. I used to make fun of people who changed their show for an American audience."

"You never thought you'd *have* an American audience," said Bobby.

"Oh, thanks a whole heap. I appreciate the vote of confidence."

It was actually kind of funny how irrational she became.

"Listen," said Bobby. "We are coming with you. We are taking the subway. We are going now. Come."

Cat raised her eyebrows at the word *come.*

"No, not you, Cat. Sorry. The rest of us. Let's go."

Kid and Bobby each took an elbow and drew Lisa to the door.

All the way to the subway, they reassured her. "This is what happens to you. You go through this every time. The show is great. It'll be fine."

They distracted her. "Look, preschoolers on a rope!"

They cajoled her. "Gary needs you. Iris needs you. The production needs you."

Lisa had doomsday answers for all of them.

For the reassurance: "I know I always say that, but *this* time is different. *This* time the show really is bad. It's got a doom-y feeling, a not-good feeling, you know? Like a Spiderman-dies-when-his-safety-line-fails feeling."

For the preschoolers on a rope: "You know what I could do with a rope? Hang myself before we ever go into previews!"

For the cajoling: "Are you kidding? This whole cast has been doing theater since they were preschoolers holding a rope! They don't need me. I'm the amateur!"

Lisa was not an amateur, but the show had started as a joke. Lisa wrote a skit with a song, "Hockey Mom," for her friend's fortieth birthday. Everyone loved it, so Lisa and Gary turned it into a Fringe Festival show. The Fringe show was a hit, so they revised and expanded and mounted it at The Lyric Theatre in Toronto. The Lyric show was a hit, so it toured. The tour was a hit, so Off-Broadway producers came calling. They were sure they could sell it in the States. But could Lisa and Gary change one little thing? Could they change it from *Hockey Mom: The Musical* to *Soccer Mom: The Musical*?

In the subway station, a man played accordion with his hands, a bugle with his mouth, a high-hat and bass drum with one leg and a string of puppets with his other leg.

"Hey, Mom. A one-man band," said Kid.

"Oh, don't remind me," Lisa said. "So many things that could go wrong."

"Mom, how is that even related?"

"*Soccer Mom: The Musical.* Is that even funny? I can't tell what's funny anymore. I'm not sure I ever knew."

"You know what would be good, Lisa?" Bobby said. They were on the subway by this time.

"What?"

"If you would stop talking."

"Bobby, talking is how I process, talking is how I

get through things. You know me. When I'm nervous, I talk. I can't help it. It's a reflex."

Lisa talked and they cajoled and reassured and distracted all the way to the rehearsal hall. There was a stagehand there to meet her at the back door.

"Lisa?" she said.

"I am," she said with a winning smile.

"I'm Wanda. It's *so nice* to meet you."

"The pleasure's all mine, Wanda."

You would never know she had whined and quivered and dragged her heels the whole way there. You had to be the people closest to her, the people standing on either side of her, in fact, to know that even now she was hesitating, holding back.

Bobby and Kid joined shoulders behind her and gave her a little push up the stairs, a nudge on the landing, slight pressure toward the door.

Aaaand *there*.

When Lisa stepped over the threshold of a theatrical space, her spine straightened, her muscles relaxed, her mind quit spinning like summer tires in the snow. She was fine.

Phew.

The door swung shut behind her. Kid and Bobby high-fived.

"What do we do now, Kid?"

The original plan had been to use their mornings for Kid's schoolwork and Bobby's playwriting. Afternoons, they'd go to museums and explore New York. But since today they were out already, it made sense to flip the arrangement.

"What's the closest museum?" Kid asked.

Bobby looked it up. "The Tenement Museum."

"Let's go," said Kid.

So they spent the morning learning what it was like to live with five kids in a small dark apartment above a beer parlor.

Back at Doug's apartment, Kid sat at the desk in her room (she loved making and stowing the Murphy bed each morning) and wrote up her observations and what she had learned. A pigeon cooed outside the window.

She wrote a postcard to her grandmother.

Dear Nanya, Today we went to the Tenement Museum. It was like going back in time. Seven people lived in two rooms with no running water. Crowded! Smelly! Outhouses in the back. One apartment had 22 layers of wallpaper. Miss you. Give Fleabag a pat for me. Love, Kid.

Bobby sat at the dining-room table with his computer. When Kid went into the kitchen to get a snack, he quickly shut the laptop and stretched, but she was pretty sure he had been watching surfing wipe-out videos.

•

Lisa came home in a completely different mood than the way she had left. You could see it in the set of her shoulders as she came into the living room where Kid was making Sudokus for Bobby to solve.

"So?" said Bobby.

"It was great. Everyone was fantastic. The star was not a diva at all. She was friendly and funny and kind. None of them were divas. None of them."

There were eight soccer moms in the play. The star played the rich one divorcing her third husband.

"See?" said Kid.

"I know. You're totally right. I'm sorry."

"Did you rehearse the opening number?" asked Bobby.

The opening number was called "Why Do We Do This?" and featured the moms all struggling to get their kids out the door to an early-morning soccer practice in the rain. Woven into it was a dance interlude that called for some tricky work with umbrellas.

"We did. It was great. Nobody lost an eye. The choreographer is a genius, I swear."

She hung her head at a sheepish angle.

"It's possible," she said, "that the show might be okay after all."

She rubbed Lucky Gumby. "Maybe."

She came and kissed each of them on the head. "Sorry for this morning."

"We forgive you," said Kid.

Lisa went for a run in Central Park with Cat, ate a big meal. Everything was fine, everything was normal. After supper, they caught another free concert, this one in the park, with actual musicians playing actual instruments.

The next morning it started all over again.

"Where are my keys? Where are my lucky keys? Do you think it'll rain? Do I need my umbrella? I'm pretty sure when the star was so nice yesterday? She was faking. I've seen it before. They start off all supportive and 'go-team!' but when things get difficult they turn all 'I-need-my-space.'"

Bob and Kid eyed each other across the table, got up with one mind and went to get their jackets.

"Where are you guys going?" said Lisa.

"Here are your keys," said Bob.

"Here's your umbrella," said Kid.

"Let's go," said Bob.

"What are you doing? Wait. I don't have my Lucky Gumby. Where's my Lucky Gumby?"

Kid dug through Lisa's knapsack. Lucky Gumby was in his usual place in the front zippered pouch. Kid dangled it in front of Lisa's eyes.

"Oh."

"Come," said Bob.

Cat jumped off the couch. "No, not you, Cat."

•

Days went on like this. Bob and Kid ferried Lisa to rehearsal, then went to the Natural History Museum or the Guggenheim or the MoMA or the library in the morning and then came home and did their work.

Well, "work." Kid genuinely did her math problems and read her books and wrote her book reports. She wrote up summaries of her trips to various museums. She took pictures and uploaded it all into a blog for her teacher.

Bobby, on the other hand, though he claimed to be working on his play, started out reading the paper online, which then progressed to watching videos of new bands he was interested in (you could tell because he put earbuds in) and then watching stunts-gone-wrong videos (you could tell because he kept smothering guffaws). When he suspected Kid was looking at him, he stroked his chin as if in thought, leaned forward, typed a few words until he thought she wasn't looking anymore and went back to surfing the Internet.

At first Kid thought she didn't miss school because it felt so much like they were on holiday. But once they settled into their routine, she still didn't miss it.

Maybe it was because of the museums. If she loved stepping into her school, if she loved the peculiar smell of seventy-year-old floors and doors, she loved stepping into museums and the peculiar non-smell of marble and atrium air even more. And while she did miss her friend Luna and her teacher, Ms. Scabernicky, she didn't miss them as much as she had thought she would.

She loved museums. She loved their large, airy rooms. She loved their glass cabinets and their neatly printed cards identifying artifacts. She loved the catalog numbers on the cards. She loved the artifacts themselves and could spend a long time looking at them from all angles.

Children in museums seemed to fall into two categories: tourists with their parents, or students with their school. The school groups were large and loud. Each group was like a single spread-out creature that crawled through the museum. A silverfish, maybe. An insect, for sure, because there were three divisions: head, thorax and abdomen. The head was made up of the interested kids, the ones hanging on the words of the tour guide. The thorax was girls comparing jewelry or showing each other things on cellphones or whispering and boys tripping each other or pushing each other into the girls. The abdomen was a grab bag of stragglers entranced by interesting artifacts, kids sneaking food or drink, kids who just didn't give a damn, and kids who were slow and sad and lonely.

Kid recognized that at home, she was sometimes in the head, sometimes in the abdomen, never in the thorax.

One day in the second week, Kid saw a kid who wasn't with a school group and whose adult, an older woman no taller than he was, did not seem like a tourist. They were peering at models of single-celled organisms. They looked familiar.

Later that afternoon, seeing their backs on the path in front of them near the reservoir in Central Park, Kid figured out why. They were in Doug's *Book of Cat*. Dr. Zinta Lomp, retired chemist and romance novelist. The boy's name was Will. His hair was longer now than in Doug's watercolor but he had the same skinny frame, the same light-brown skin. They had tennis rackets slung over their shoulders. Dr. Lomp wore white tennis shoes and a raincoat.

Cat burst from the undergrowth just ahead of the pair with something in her mouth.

"Cat!" cried Will.

Cat waddled up to him, wagging her rear end.

"Catherine the Terrible!" Dr. Zinta Lomp admonished her. Cat dropped a dead rat at her feet. Dr. Lomp looked around. "Where is Doug?"

"England," said Kid, but her gaze was down.

Bob jogged up to them and clipped the leash on Cat's collar. "I'm Doug's cousin, Bob, and this is my daughter, Kid."

Kid was smacked again with a hot face, fast heartbeat, inability to look at faces and a desire to flee, or at least hide.

She breathed. She let the word *calm* sort of fall down through her mind like a magic dust.

"Hi," she managed to squeak.

They all stood there for a minute, looking at the rat.

"Right," said Bob. He handed the leash to Kid and dug plastic gloves and a poo bag out of the satchel. "I'm picking up a ..." he bent down "... lovely ..." reached out "... innocent ..." and turned his head away "... creature that just happened ..." as his hand hovered over the rat's body, unsure where to pick it up from "... to be killed by my cousin's equally innocent ..." his fingers closed around the middle of the rat "... dog."

He lifted it and held it away from him, suddenly doing a dance, lifting his knees high and wincing and shouting, "Augh! Augh! Augh!" He flapped the poo bag in the other hand, but it wouldn't stay open and he kept dancing around in a circle with the rat hand chasing the bag hand but never quite catching up.

"Peter's sake!" said Dr. Lomp. "Here."

She grabbed the bag and held it open while Bob dropped the rat in. The tail flopped over the bag's top edge, so she jiggled the bag until it fell in, then firmly knotted the top two bag corners.

Bob, meanwhile, was gasping and shuddering.

"I'm sorry, I'm sorry," he said, bent over. "I just ... hhhlgh ... really don't like rats."

"I thought it was kind of cute," said Will.

Me, too, thought Kid.

Dr. Lomp held the bag out to Kid and nodded toward a garbage can.

"Run. Put this in the trash," she said. "It is not cute. It is a rat."

"So you are Doug's cousin," said Dr. Lomp. "How do you do?"

"Great. Yeah. Fine. Awesome. I'm not always like this."

"I am Dr. Lomp. This is Will."

"Dow you do who?" said Will. He had a high voice that was a little bit grating.

"Great," said Bob again. "Sorry, what?"

"Will follows the Reverend Spooner," said Dr. Lomp.

"You reverse the initial sounds of words," Will elaborated.

Dr. Lomp began walking again. They all followed.

Will turned to Kid with an about-to-question air.

Don't-ask-me-don't-ask-me-don't-ask-me, she mentally intoned.

And he didn't. He looked ahead again.

Phew. Maybe they could just walk in silence.

Then he turned and asked, "I like Egyptology and basketball. What do you like?"

CALM, thought Kid.

"That's my opening conversational gambit," he went on. "Does it work?"

Kid tried to answer but there were no words. Just blood in her ears. Just her fast heart.

"I guess not. You're not answering."

"I ..." Kid managed to say, "like cat — " She meant to say "cats," but only "cat" came out.

"I like Cat, too."

Cat wagged her tail.

Ahead of them, the grown-ups asked each other questions with ease. Where's Doug, we're from Toronto, are you a medical doctor, tennis? Kid listened with one ear.

"What else do you like?" asked Will.

"England!" she said, followed by a fresh rush of hot-face. She had never been to England. What if he wanted to talk about it?

"What do you like about England?"

"You know," she said vaguely. "Engl ... ish ... things."

"Like?"

"I don't know ..." She tried to think of English things.

"You like England, but you don't know what you like about it?"

"Tea?" she said. "Castles?"

This seemed to satisfy him.

"I saw you in the museum," said Will. "Are you homeschooled, too?"

"Correspondence," said Kid. "I'm doing correspondence. From Toronto. Where we're from."

They walked in silence for a while. The heat in her face faded. Kid felt she should ask him something.

"Have you always been homeschooled?"

"Yes. My parents died in the Twin Towers. Bubcha won't let me out of her sight."

"Oh," she said. What else do you say when someone says his parents died in the Twin Towers? Maybe nothing. Maybe you wait and let them say more and if they don't you change the subject.

Suddenly a little social anxiety didn't seem like such a big deal.

She waited. Will didn't say anything more.

Right. Time to change the subject. She heard her mom's voice in her head. *You can do it, Kid.*

"I thought I'd miss school, but I don't. Not so far. Maybe when I get bored I'll miss it. Do you miss it?"

She made a mental note to ask her parents about the Twin Towers. All she really knew was that they'd fallen and that the tenth anniversary had just passed.

"Never had it. How could I miss it?"

"What about other kids?"

Will shrugged. "Other kids don't usually like me. Are you staying in ugg's department?"

Kid's brain did a little hiccup while reversing the initial sounds of the two words. Doug's apartment, he meant. She nodded. She wanted to ask why other kids didn't like him, but didn't want to be rude.

"Have you geen the soat yet?" Will asked.

Another hiccup.

"What goat?"

"They say there's a gountain moat that lives on top of your building. But the goat is very secretive. No one ever sees it. Hardly anyone. They say if you see it, you have seven gears of lewd yuck."

"Seven gears of lewd yuck?"

"Seven years of good luck."

"Have you seen it?"

Will shook his head. "I can't look out windows. I get dizzy and throw up and fall down. It's a form of agoraphobia."

Kid was curious. "Can you look *at* windows?"

"It's hard to look at them without looking through them. But yes. At night. For short periods of time. Makes me feel queasy and nervous, though. I don't like mirrors much, either."

"Oh."

They parted at the tennis courts.

"Well. They're interesting, eh?" said Bobby.

"I'll say. Will says there's a goat that lives on Doug's building."

"A goat?"

"A mountain goat. He said if you see it, you get seven gears of lewd yuck."

"Who would want seven gears of lewd yuck?"

"Seven years of good luck."

"I wouldn't even want one gear of lewd yuck. I had enough lewd yuck with that rat to last me seven gears."

Kid punched her dad on the arm.

He punched her back. "How would a mountain goat get on Doug's building?"

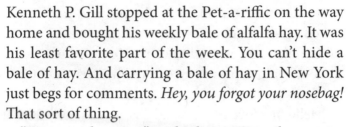

Kenneth P. Gill stopped at the Pet-a-riffic on the way home and bought his weekly bale of alfalfa hay. It was his least favorite part of the week. You can't hide a bale of hay. And carrying a bale of hay in New York just begs for comments. *Hey, you forgot your nosebag!* That sort of thing.

"Hamsters hungry?" said Julio as Kenneth came in.

"They're guinea pigs," said Kenneth. "And they don't eat it, they sleep in it."

As he waited for the elevator doors to close, a rumpled-looking man and a skinny kid with long hair and a ball cap came in with the dog named Cat. He held the elevator for them.

"Thanks," said the man.

"Where's Doug?" asked Kenneth.

"England," said the kid, looking at his shoulder.

Did he have dandruff? He brushed his shoulders just in case.

"We're looking after Cat for him," said the man.

"Ah. I have guinea pigs. Two of them. Wallace and Pita."

Kenneth had that funny feeling in his stomach that came with lying. Why had he offered that information? They hadn't asked. Obviously he was lying. Why is that man lying? they were thinking. He has the hay for some other reason that he is hiding, I just know it.

His throat got tight.

Luckily, they got off before he did and he was relieved when he got off the elevator that there were no other neighbors around to lie to. He called out to his fictional guinea pigs as he entered his apartment just the same.

"Hello, my lovelies," he said. "How was your day?"

Meantime he scouted around. Had the goat come in today?

No. Of course not.

He got out the scissors, snipped the string around one end of the bale, filled the bucket and put it out on the ledge.

The goat would not come until dusk when he felt the smallest bit safe. Kenneth would try to coax him back into the apartment, although what he would do if he succeeded he was not at all certain.

He needed a big crate. It would take a big crate to move a mountain goat. And it would have to be strong. And have holes in it. And be on wheels so he could take it down the hall to the freight elevator and

down the elevator and out the back door to a ... van
or truck or something. A van or truck that he could
drive across the country to the mountains ... after
phoning into work ... with a ... medical emergency.

As soon as the goat came back in through the window, he would swing into action.

Swing! Instantly.

In the meantime, la la la. Goat? What goat? I have
hamsters. I mean guinea pigs. Named Wallace. And
Pita.

The goat woke in the near dark to a faint, wondrous
smell. It drew him to his feet, led him to the ledge.

There. It came from over there, past the gray river
of moving clumps. There, where the tree smell came
from. There, where hope lay.

Grass.

Saliva flooded his mouth. He *had* to brave the
clangy cliff. Now.

He trotted to the other side of his sad little mountain.

No point wasting time. He leapt. With his footpads
out, there was only the slightest clang as he landed.
Then, before he knew it, he was *not* going down the
clangy cliff but taking his usual route ledge to ledge
to the bucket.

Why?

Oh.

Hay. Hay was good.

Why had he been thinking of going down the clangy cliff? Had there been a smell?

There had. A really good smell. He should really find it again. He should …

Mmm, hay. He was at the hay. He was eating the hay.

The goat didn't know much. But he knew these things:

Danger comes from above.

Danger comes from below.

Gamboling is the purest state of being.

Hunger is constant.

Choose the closest path to food.

Don't let hunger fool you. You're still in danger.

He bristled. There beyond the bucket was the face of the tree-ish creature that wanted to trap him and keep him in the cave.

The hay was a trap! Leap away, leap away!

3

In the same way that in the week after you look up a word you've never encountered before you're sure to see it three or four times, Kid kept running into the tiny woman and the kid from the park.

First she spotted them at the Guggenheim, side by side on a big round seat, each gazing at a different abstract painting. They didn't turn their heads, and Kid ducked out of the room, steering her father to the next gallery.

Then she saw them in the checkout line at the fruit store on Amsterdam Avenue. They didn't see her then, either. She bent her head so her ball cap covered her face just in case.

The day after that, they were again in the park on their way to play tennis, too far away to call out to.

Then Kid didn't see them at all for a while and she forgot about them.

She was getting used to the apartment and the city. She didn't notice the taste of the water anymore. Her hand got used to the heft of the glasses. She knew how to get to the subway station. She could say hello to the jogging grandma. Whenever they saw the man with the rainbow yarmulke, they did their best to speak in chorus.

She couldn't look anyone in the eye yet. But she would. Sometime. Probably.

She did, in fact, start to miss school. Not a lot. But a little. She missed people her age. She missed Luna.

Lisa did not need to be taken to rehearsals anymore. Kid and Bobby could go straight to their museum of choice in the mornings.

Lately, Bobby had made actual progress on his play and had taken to finding a spot in the museum cafeteria to work while Kid went off and explored on her own. She had a good sense of direction and a map and there were security guards in almost every room. It was safe.

Kid was just starting on a self-directed tour of the first floor of the Metropolitan Museum of Art. The first stop was an Egyptian tomb.

She walked through a gap in a massive limestone wall and across a courtyard, then into a narrow passage. She turned a corner and another corner.

And there were Will and Dr. Lomp. Right there in the little stone room.

There was no ducking and turning away this time.

"Mood gorning," said Will.

"Oh," said Kid.

Dr. Lomp had headphones on. She smiled and nodded her head, tapped the headphones and turned back to the designs on the wall.

"Welcome to Perneb's tomb," said Will. He gestured as if it were his home.

Kid's mouth caught up to her brain.

"Hi," she said, looking at the wall behind him. An Egyptian carried a string of fish.

"This might be my favorite place in the whole city," said Will.

The stone was very warm in color and there was a lot to look at, though the room was not large. If Kid and Will and Dr. Lomp stood shoulder to shoulder, they would cover its breadth, and if they lay down head to toe, they would probably cover its length. The walls were full of sideways-facing Egyptians, like the fish carrier, doing stuff.

"This is the offering room," said Will. "That door." He pointed at the wall at the end with vertical slabs on either side of a recessed center. "That's where Perneb's spirit enters, or would if he were here. He's back in Egypt. His mummy is. The actual burial chamber would have been down a deep shaft, about as deep as the building is tall. And his family would come to bring him offerings. And he'd come up the shaft and through that door, and they could eat together and hang out."

Now Kid could see that some of the people on the walls were pouring drinks or carrying dishes or carrying animals. It was amazing how much carving there was and how much detail.

Will said, "When they brought the tomb here from Egypt, they didn't bring the burial chamber. I'm assuming it's still back there. Sometimes I wonder if Perneb's spirit comes up in Egypt now and goes, *Whoa, where am I? Where's the house I built for my afterlife?* Or maybe his spirit did that the first time it came up, and then because there was no tomb there anymore, it went soaring up into the air and started wandering the earth looking for its tomb."

"Or it just went exploring," said Kid. "Like, *Ooh, hey, check out the pyramids. I remember those. Wait a minute, what's over here? What are those weird tall buildings?*"

"Let me show you the other room," said Will. He led Kid back out to the courtyard and over to another narrow door leading to another narrow room. Dr. Lomp trailed along behind them.

This room was dimmer. There was a small museum cabinet they didn't pay attention to because in this room your eyes were drawn to the far wall, to the tall, narrow castle-window-like slit with brightness beyond it.

Up close you could see, lit from above, another room, square, with a statue of Perneb seated in the middle.

"There he is," said Will.

Kid remembered Will saying he couldn't look through windows. But he was looking through this one. An indoor window. That looked indoors. At Perneb.

"He's there," said Will. "You can see him. But you can never reach him. You can never touch him. That's the point."

They stayed there for quite a while, just looking through the window. It was very peaceful gazing upon Perneb in the warm light in his own room. People came and went behind them. And then, when they had had enough, they turned to go.

By then — Kid could not have said exactly when or how — the shyness barrier had been broken. She could look at Will, she could look him in the eyes (they were brown), she could laugh, she could talk.

Will showed her his favorite pieces in the cabinet. A comb carved with animal figures. A small statue of Horus, the falcon-headed god.

They wandered easily through the rest of the Egyptian exhibit, breaking apart to follow their interests, coming back together again, calling one another over to look at particular things, imagining what it would have been like to be alive four thousand years ago.

Dr. Lomp trailed them, listening to whatever was on her headphones.

Eventually, Kid's watch beeped.

"That's my signal to go meet Dad."

"We're here every Tuesday," said Will.

•

That evening, Kid's mom came through the door, dropped her bags with a clunk and said, "Previews start in three weeks! Previews! Off Broadway!"

She bugged her eyes out and sucked her chin in. Then she staggered forward and fell onto the couch. Cat licked her face. Bob patted her back.

Kid sang, "Oh, Mo-om, you're a funny one, with a nose like a pickled oni-on," which almost always cheered Lisa up.

Cat sang along. "Roo roo-roo, roo roo-oo, roo roo roo roo roo-roo."

Who doesn't love a singing dog?

Lisa, apparently. She remained catatonic.

"Your legs are like toothpicks, but we still love you."

They tried telling her it would be fine, the show was great, she knew it was great, they knew it was great, it did great in Toronto for eighteen months, it did great in Chicago, it was going to do great in New York.

They tried telling her even if it got crappy reviews and closed in a week, wasn't she always the one saying failure was necessary and how one learned? Wasn't she the one always saying you cannot take these things personally? You strike a chord with gazillions of people or you strike a chord with two. Doesn't make the show any better or worse.

They reminded her how good the advance press had been.

They offered to order takeout, normally a sure-fire way of perking her up.

Nothing. She stared morosely across the room at the legs of Doug's drawing board.

"This is why I got out of theater," said Bob.

"Hey, Mom," said Kid. "What happened with the Twin Towers?"

"What?"

"Will said his parents died in the Twin Towers."

Bob and Lisa exchanged Significant Parent Glances, and Lisa patted Kid's hand, and Cat cocked her head, and Bob sat down beside Lisa, and then they were telling the story.

"I was voicing a skunk for an animated series," said Lisa. "So I was in the studio."

"And I was looking after you," said Bob. "You were not quite two. It was a beautiful day. September eleventh. Didn't even really feel like fall yet. I had you out in the stroller."

"I'm in the middle of my lines, I'm in this booth. The director's in another booth, and she stops me, she says something's happened. She leaves the booth. So I follow her. We go to the reception area where there's a TV and on the TV there's a plane flying into an office building. Like right into it."

"You fell asleep in the stroller," said Bob. "And I brought you home and carried the whole stroller up the stairs and left you in it because you always used to wake up when we took you out of the stroller and then the phone rang and I answered it really fast because I didn't want it to wake you — "

"And it was me. Because we were all feeling like we had to call the people we loved and say, 'Go turn on the TV. Something's happened. I can't explain. Go turn on the TV.'"

Kid's parents' faces were still and serious and sort of haunted. She looked back and forth between them as they spoke.

"So I turned on the TV," said Bobby. "And I saw the same thing. A plane. Flying into a huge office tower. The World Trade Center in New York."

"What was going on? We didn't know. Nobody knew. Was it an accident? Was it deliberate?" Lisa let out a long breath, and they both paused before Bobby spoke again.

"It was deliberate."

Lisa went on. "And then a second plane hit the other tower. The twin. Firefighters arrived. They started evacuating. People were getting out of the buildings. They were streaming out. And the firefighters were going in."

"And people got out as fast as they could, but not everyone could get out before the towers fell. These were really tall buildings. The only way out was the stairs."

Kid could feel her heart beating way up high in her chest.

"So the buildings fell. They collapsed," said Lisa. "Almost three thousand people died."

Including Will's parents, Kid thought. Will must have been somewhere else. At daycare. Or with his grandmother.

"Who would do that?" Kid asked.

Her parents looked at each other again.

"People who want to spread fear," said her dad. "Terrorists. People who want people to be so afraid that they will do what the terrorists want."

"But that's not a real answer," said Lisa.

"No," said Bob.

Kid's parents hugged her from either side. They made a Kid sandwich.

Kid thought about how she'd both known and not known about the disaster. People talked about it all the time. *After nine-eleven*, they said. She'd never fully taken it in.

But Will had fully taken it in. He had known about it his whole life.

How easily he had said, "My parents died in the Twin Towers."

Kid had not slept with her parents in a long time, but she slept with them that night. She felt like she had had a nightmare, only she was sadder than when she had nightmares.

Her parents were warm barriers on either side of her. None of them slept very well. They were too squished. But they were together.

Plus, Kid's mom wasn't worried about the opening of her show anymore.

Marek and Martin rode their ATVs along the fault. Where were all the robots? They were gone. It was a mystery. A boring boring mystery that nobody cared about.

Backspace backspace backspace backspace.

"What's going on?" shouted Mara.

Whoops. Backspace.

"What's going on?" shouted Marek.

Suddenly …

Joff sighed, hand poised over his Braille writer.

The Plates of Barifna was terrible. It was boring, it was wooden. Wood was fine for tables. He knocked on his table. Wood was fine for dogs to chew on. He patted Michigan's head. Wood was fine for puppets.

A lonely wooden puppet.

That had once been a prop in *The Sound of Music* and gathered dust on a collector's shelf until it was eventually auctioned off. The bidding was fierce between an agent for a blind fantasy/sci-fi writer and a honey-voiced, um, hedge-fund manager? Actor/waitress? Lab technician? Puppeteer/waitress named, say, Mara.

`"Think you're going to win this, bucka-roo?" Mara muttered as she raised her bidding paddle yet again. "Think again."`

Joff leaned back in his chair. Maybe he'd meet Larry for lunch. Maybe he'd go to the library.

But he didn't go to the library. He went to Washington Square. When people yelled at him as he rolled past, he said, "Same to you, buckaroo," and smiled.

He got there around two in the afternoon and played chess with Ginger and Mikael and Chili.

"Hey, you know that woman I played a couple of days ago?" he asked.

"The one with the Afro?"

"She had an Afro?"

"You like her, Joff?"

"Joffey likes her!"

"Joffey's got a girlfriend, Joffey's got a crush."

"I just want to know, has anybody seen her before."

Nobody had seen her before or since. Joff worried she'd been a tourist. That she'd gone back to wherever she lived.

He couldn't place her accent. Not Southern, at least. She wasn't from Florida or Texas or Alabama or Louisiana. Although just because you were from somewhere didn't mean you still lived there. She could have grown up in Minneapolis and moved to Florida. She could have been born in Holland like Joff and moved to Vermont when she was two, and then lived in Michigan from six to fourteen.

Joff wished he'd asked Mara more about herself. What her job was, where she lived, how often she came to play chess. Playing chess was more than a one-time thing, obviously, since she'd talked about the players who thought she was an easy win. Joff wanted to hear her say "buckaroo." He wanted to hear her talk to Michigan in a little talking-to-dogs voice. He wanted to play chess with her. He wanted to …

He just wanted to see her again.

That's all.

Maybe she would be back the next day.

Joff was.

And the day after that. And the day after that. And the day after that.

Back at the museum the day after she met Will at Perneb's tomb, Kid spent the morning in the European Art section. When she went to the museum cafeteria to meet Bobby, she found him watching stock-car-racing videos on his computer.

"Oh, hey, Kid," he said.

"Racing videos?" she said.

"Research," he said.

"Bobby," she said. "Do you really *want* to work on this play?"

"Of course I do."

"Because when Mom works on a play, she, like, doesn't do anything else. She wanders around shouting in other people's voices. Even when she's doing the laundry — "

"We're different, okay?" he said. "We are not the same people."

"Okay, Bobby. I just thought you might be happier if you — "

"What? If I gave up? I am not a quitter, Kid. You are not looking at a quitter. And stop calling me Bobby."

They headed home, back across the park. Kid led the way, map in hand, scouting out new routes so eventually they'd get to know its whole expanse. Today's route took them past the castle and the Shakespeare Garden and wound along curving treed paths.

Then, suddenly, through the trees appeared a clear view of Doug's building.

Could there really be a goat living on it?

There was no sign of one right now, but a façade atop the building obscured view of the penthouse. If it obscured view of the penthouse, it could definitely obscure view of the goat.

Was there a goat?

It didn't make any sense.

It wasn't logical.

But Kid was going to look. She was going to look every day.

If there is a goat, she thought, I'm going to find it.

Her mom needed good luck. Her dad needed good luck. Maybe she did, too.

Who didn't, when it came down to it.

•

At first, Kid's search for the goat was idle and random. Building scans as they came back from the park or the subway. A window check after lunch or between blogging and math. She got quite familiar with a timid white pigeon that liked to roost on the ledge outside her bedroom window.

"Hello, Ovid," she said to the pigeon, the name popping into her head for no reason. "Aren't you the scaredy pigeon?"

But she didn't see any goat.

She decided to be more systematic. She made a chart. Which window, what time of day and length of watch.

There were several methods of looking out the window. She could open the window and stick her head right out. This was her preferred method, as it gave the greatest building coverage.

The building was twelve stories tall. Running below the windows on each floor was a ledge maybe ten inches wide. Good footing for a goat. Running around the eleventh floor was a significantly wider ledge. Great footing for a goat.

At first she planned twenty-minute watches at one-hour intervals, but it was hard to stay vigilant. After you watched for twenty minutes, the idea that a goat might live and leap on the ledges seemed ridiculous.

Besides, there were other things to watch — people on the street, the frightened white pigeon on the ledge, cyclists, Joff on his skateboard, a man on a stand-up electric scooter, people in the park.

Kid also wondered whether head-out-the-window might deter the goat from venturing within sight. So her second method was the oblique method.

She would stand a foot to one side of a window and peer out to see as much ledge as possible. She would do this quietly, unexpectedly, at various times of day.

On her third day of watching, about five o'clock in the afternoon, Ovid launched his scrawny butt off the ledge and flew not twenty feet from the building when a falcon, who must have been perched on the roof of the building opposite, dove and taloned the pigeon.

"You were right, Ovid. It is a big scary world out there," Kid whispered.

But then she thought about the falcon, how it was made to do what it did and had no choice in the matter. It was eat pigeon (or sparrow or rat or raccoon) or die, and Kid supposed that the beauty of the falcon was directly related to its ability to kill, a completely different kind of beauty than the beauty of the pigeon, and that humans' ability to recognize the two beauties and not to call one beautiful and the other ugly said a lot about humans in ways you could probably spend years contemplating.

•

The next day was Tuesday.

"Let's go to the Met," said Kid. She wanted to see Will.

"All right," said Bobby.

Will was in Perneb's tomb, just as he said he'd be.

"Hell, wello," he said with a big smile. "Coo yame!"

Kid smiled back. "Yow are who?"

"Wery vell, yank thoo."

Dr. Lomp, again wearing headphones, acknowledged Kid with a nod.

Will sort of basked in the air of the room.

"Doesn't it make you feel calm and at ease?"

Kid shrugged. "I guess."

While Will communed or whatever it was he was

doing, Kid examined the walls, with their processions of Egyptians bringing things to Perneb. One of them was a goat, she was pretty sure, and another was a goose, and a lamb.

"Come on," said Will.

As before, they moved to the other room, the one with the window that allowed you to look through to a seated Perneb, lit as if by the sun.

Kid tried to imagine it wasn't Perneb she was visiting but Bobby or Lisa. If she imagined Lisa as the statue, it would stay still for about a half second and then do something goofy to make Kid laugh — pick her teeth or pretend to fart.

A seated Bobby statue was even harder to imagine. She could only half see him in Perneb's pose, and when she did, a yawning feeling arose in her chest, an emptiness bigger than she knew. She banished the feeling and told herself the statue was Perneb. Perneb and no one else.

Again Kid and Will turned away from Perneb as with one mind. Will led Kid through a different set of rooms in the Egyptian wing. At the end of one of them, he stopped her and said, "The Temple of Dendur is through there. You should go see it. I'll wait for you here."

She looked at him questioningly.

"Windows," he said. "You'll see."

She did. Windows made up one whole giant wall of the space, which also included a sort of moat separating plaza from temple.

Kid was puzzled by Will's fear. The room was not high up. It was on the ground floor. All you saw through the windows were trees with the very first hints of fall colors and greenery.

To her, being in the room was almost exactly like being outside. Why be scared of that?

Why be unable to look people in the eye? said a voice in her head. Why turn into a rabbit when asked a question?

She turned back to Will. They went on to the Arms and Armor section, and then American Art, and then her watch beeped. It was time to go meet Bobby.

"Hey," said Will. "Want to join us for a picnic? We usually eat outside if it's warm enough and then go to Ground Zero to leave an offering."

Ground Zero. That was the term her parents had used to talk about the site of the collapsed World Trade Center towers.

"I'll ask Bobby," said Kid.

Will and Dr. Lomp came with her to the cafeteria, and Bobby said sure and grabbed them a couple of sandwiches. They ate on a park bench in the sunshine.

"Every Tuesday," said Dr. Lomp, "we go to the World Trade Center and remember Will's parents."

"Want to come?" said Will.

Kid and Bobby looked at each other and nodded.

"Sure," said Kid.

They packed up and started walking.

"They met in the elevator at work," said Will. "They used to smile at each other before they even knew each other's names."

"He was a software engineer," said Dr. Lomp.

"And she was a web designer."

Will and Dr. Lomp continued to tell them about Will's parents — she played electric guitar, he used to figure skate, she liked brownies, he liked comic books — as they walked to the subway and rode to the site where the towers had been. They explained that a memorial was being built. It would be two great square holes in the ground on the footprint of the two towers, two four-sided waterfalls descending into deep square pools, with another square in the middle.

"Like an Egyptian burial shaft," said Will.

Wow, thought Kid. Wow.

Kid would have thought from looking at it that Ground Zero was just a huge construction site. Chain-link fence covered in gauzy green see-through material bounded the area. Four cranes worked away at unknown tasks. Across the way a new tower was partly built.

They walked next to the fence while Dr. Lomp pointed out where the original buildings had stood, and which buildings around them had been damaged when they fell.

Will took a brownie from a ziplock bag in his pocket, kissed it and chucked it over the fence.

"Hey!" a large woman in an orange sweater shouted at him. "Whaddaya doing hucking garbage in there?"

"I am making an offering to my parents," Will said calmly. "They died here nine years ago."

"Oh, sweetie!" the woman said. "I am so sorry!"

She moved forward.

"Please do not hug me," said Will. But Dr. Lomp had already put herself between the would-be hugger and Will. The woman had her hand to her mouth and was sprouting tears. Dr. Lomp waved her away, and she turned and left them.

Others passed by without comment as Will rolled up a comic book, bent down and stuffed it through one of the bottom diamonds of chain-link. He stood with both hands on the fence, facing it. He gave off the same feeling as he did in the room with Perneb, a kind of charged serenity.

Bobby took Kid's hand.

Then Will was done. They walked a circuit around the site. The enormity of what had happened when she and Will were babies hit Kid all over again.

They were silent on the ride uptown, but as they parted at the subway station, Bobby said, "Thanks for that," and Kid added her own thanks.

"We're going to the Cloisters tomorrow," said Will. "Want to come?"

"Sure," said Kid.

"Absolutely," said Bobby.

As they approached home, Kid walked on the other side of the street to get a better view of the top of Doug's building and craned her neck.

But there was still no goat. Not that she could see.

•

The Cloisters, up in Washington Heights, by the Hudson River, was a fake monastery that included a series of connected square gardens enclosed within walls with covered walkways. It was based on actual medieval cloisters in Europe.

Dr. Lomp gave them a tour of the gardens, pointing out the different plants and what they were used for — some for pigment in painting, some for medicine, some for cooking — and which chemical compounds made them effective.

"Yow are who?" whispered Kid.

"Bot nad," said Will.

The day was warm with a ground note of chill. A lone butterfly wove an erratic path through the air. Bobby lapped up Dr. Lomp's commentary, peppering her with questions. Kid took many notes. Will sketched plants in a sketchbook, then touched them up with watercolor paints. He offered a sheet of watercolor paper and a spare brush to Kid. They very happily whiled away the morning.

As they were wrapping up to go, Bobby asked if they would like to come over for lunch.

Dr. Lomp and Will exchanged a look.

"That is very kind," said Dr. Lomp. "But — "

"Do you have blinds on your windows?" said Will.

"Yes," said Bobby, surprised. Kid had never told him about Will and windows.

"Do you mind pulling them down before I come in? I can't look out of windows."

"We can do that," said Bobby.

"Then yes," said Dr. Lomp. "We would like that very much."

As they walked home from the subway, Kid said to Will, "I've leen booking gor the foat."

"Lo nuck?"

"Yot net."

Like Kid had done the day before, they stood as far from Doug's building as possible to give them the best angle of the rooftop.

No goat.

They cut down the alley behind the building and looked up from there.

Nothing on the fire escape. Nothing on the roofline.

"The goat does not want to be seen," said Dr. Lomp as they headed inside. Julio was on the door. "There is only so much luck to go around. The goat cannot be seen by everyone."

"Have you seen the goat?" asked Kid. The elevator opened and they stepped on.

"My friend Herschel has seen the goat," said Dr. Lomp.

Will said, "Didn't Herschel fall and break his hip?"

"Yes."

"That's not very good luck, is it?"

"He is old. Maybe he was lucky to live."

Kid realized Dr. Lomp had not answered whether she herself had seen the goat. She did not say she had. She did not say she had not.

Kid asked again.

"I am not interested in looking for the goat," Dr. Lomp said. "What would I do with good luck now? I do not need it. I have had good fortune. I have had bad. I escaped a troubled country and came here. I was lucky. I had not very much money. I was unlucky. I met a man and fell in love and married him. I was lucky. We had two children. I was lucky. My husband died. I was unlucky. My son married and had a son. I was lucky. My son and daughter-in-law died. I was unlucky. My grandson is alive. I am lucky. I believe in the goat but I do not believe in luck."

The elevator door opened at their floor. Will began to hum. Dr. Lomp put a hand on his shoulder. Bobby turned right and led them to the apartment.

"Wait right here," he said, opening the door. Kid ducked in after him. Cat whumped her tail against the floor. They pulled down the blinds on each of the windows and turned on the lights.

Will had his hands up by his eyes like blinkers. He moved hesitantly, stopped, slowly let his hands down and sighed a big breath out.

"Thanks. I think I'm okay now."

"It is not easy to accept invitations," said Dr. Lomp.

After lunch, Bobby showed Dr. Lomp what he had written on his play so far. She sat at the dining-room table, leafing through the pages he'd printed, a serious expression on her face. Bobby looked at his phone and snuck mini-glances at her. Her face gave nothing away.

Kid and Will took turns trying to maneuver a small ball bearing through a three-dimensional obstacle course inside a clear plastic sphere.

"Do you really think there's a goat?" Kid asked Will. Her ball bearing dropped. She passed the sphere over.

Will shrugged. "Stranger things have happened. If there is, then someone must have seen it, don't you think? You should ask around."

Will was exceptionally good at the game. He'd already made it ten moves past the point where Kid kept getting stuck.

"I'll just keep looking on my own," she said.

"The more people you ask, the more likely you'll

find someone who's seen it. We could ask Herschel, but he's still in hospital."

"I'm not much of an ask-around type."

"What do you mean?"

"I'm shy."

"You are?"

"Yeah."

"I would never have known."

Kid shrugged.

"Do you get, like, dizzy, and pass out?" said Will.

"I get really hot and my heart goes fast and it's like there's this force keeping my head from looking at people and I want to hide."

"Huh," said Will. "What if I go with you?"

"I don't know."

Will said, "We're going to practice with the door-man."

He very gradually tipped the sphere so the ball bearing tripped down a shallow set of stairs.

"We are?"

"You are."

"When?"

"Bubcha," Will called out. "We're going to go ask the doorman if he's seen the goat."

"I am almost done," said Dr. Lomp, holding up her finger.

Will was still manipulating the sphere. He had now made it three-quarters of the way through.

Dr. Lomp turned the last page. "Done."

"Well?" said Bobby. He looked like a puppy.

Will put down the sphere. The ball bearing dropped.

"Let's go," said Will.

Dr. Lomp got up.

"Can't they go on their own?" said Bobby. "It's just the lobby."

"No," said Dr. Lomp. "We will be back."

Will had really meant it when he said that his grandmother didn't let him out of her sight.

Kid started getting nervous in the elevator. By the time the door opened, she could feel her heart pulsing in her throat.

Will, she noticed, had his head down and his hand shielding his eyes from the sight of the front door.

Julio sat on a stool behind a counter, reading a newspaper and eating a sandwich. Kid crept up beside him. She let the word *calm* float down through her again.

"Um," said Kid, looking at Julio's shoes. "Excuse me."

Julio turned. "What can I do you for, Kid?"

Kid made herself flick her eyes up and down. He had something on his chin. Mustard, maybe.

"Have you ever, uh," said Kid. "Have you ever heard a rumor that there's a goat on our building?"

"A what?"

"A goat."

"Like with four legs and horns and a beard?"

"Yeah."

"A goat. On the building. Are we talking about the same thing here?"

"I think so. If you see it, you get seven years of good luck."

"Oh, *that* rumor." He rolled his eyes. Or at least he used the same voice people use when they roll their eyes. "Of course I have not heard that rumor. That's a crazy rumor. How would a goat get on our building? Oh, wait. Hey. You're trying to get my goat, aren't you?" He slapped his leg.

Will said, "I think you've got some mustard on your chin."

Julio wiped his chin with the heel of his hand.

"Thanks, anyway," said Kid. Her temples were damp, her hands clammy. Like the word *calm* had got mixed up on its float downwards and had come out *clam*.

But she had done it. She had asked.

Back in the apartment, Dr. Lomp told Bobby she thought his play was not about two brothers and the car they were fixing up at all but about their father.

"He is going to steal the car, isn't he?" she said. "I can see it coming. It is brilliant."

Bobby's eyes went wide. "It *is* brilliant."

Kid showed Will her room and her Murphy bed and her goat-finding chart.

"You know what we need to do," he said. "Survey the building. Ask everyone. Bubcha," he called out, heading back to the living room. "We're going to survey the building to see if anyone has seen the goat."

"Now you are going to do this?"

"Yeah."

"What do you mean, survey?" Bobby asked.

"We're going to knock on doors and ask them, 'Have you seen the goat?'"

"We are?" said Kid.

"We are."

"Where do we start?" said Dr. Lomp.

Kid sighed. "I'll get my clipboard," she said.

"Wait, you're going, too?" Bobby said to Dr. Lomp.

"I go where Will goes," she said.

Kid got her clipboard and pen. She and Will headed down the hall, Will shading his eyes from the window at the end. Dr. Lomp trailed behind them.

There were eight apartments on their floor.

Kid knocked at the first door. Her heart raced, then slowed a little when nobody answered. She started to move away.

"Not so fast," said Will. He knocked again. A faint thumping sound came from the apartment.

At last, a large older woman with a cane opened the door. She wore baggy clothes and seemed covered in dust or maybe flour.

Will poked Kid.

Her mouth felt dry. It opened and closed. Her head was turning away of its own accord.

"Hi," she said nonetheless. "We're your neighbors. Well, I am. This is my friend, Will. We're … what are we doing, Will?"

Will had his head down and his hands over his eyes like blinkers again.

"We're conducting a survey," he said.

"I'm not interested," said the woman.

"No, it's not like that," said Will, but the woman was already closing the door.

"Have you seen a goat on our building?" Kid called through the narrowing gap.

Thud. The door closed.

"That went well," said Will.

Kid laughed, suddenly giddy. Will laughed with her. They ran to the next door.

There was no answer at any of the other doors except the last one, which was opened by a young woman in sweatpants with cotton between her bright green toenails.

Kid managed to focus on her chin. It was moving. She was eating a piece of toast.

"Hi," said Kid. "We've heard a rumor that a goat lives on our building, and we're doing a survey to see if anybody has seen it."

"I'm sorry, what?"

Kid repeated herself. Will shielded his eyes.

The woman laughed high. She laughed low. "You're asking me if I have seen a goat on our building."

"That's right."

"No, come on, you're just — "

"Ma'am, I assure you, we are a hundred percent serious," said Will from behind his hand-binoculars.

"Um, no," she said.

"Thank you for your time," said Will.

They gave up for the day, went back to the apartment and played backgammon.

On Monday, Doris picked up her mail on the way in from Seniors Helping Sophomores. She had left Jonathan pretending to play a game on his iPad — wheatgrass drink and rye crackers on his side table. She came home to find him asleep in his chair, the wheatgrass undrunk.

The sight of him asleep filled her with tenderness. She rested on the arm of his chair and kissed his head. He roused, briefly relaxing against her before stiffening, harrumphing.

He began a message on the iPad. Doris let herself hope that today was the day he got over things and just got back to being Jonathan.

I, he wrote.

"Yes, Jojo," she said expectantly.

Have, he wrote.

"I have," she repeated.

To pee, he finished.

Oh, boy. That was not communication.

"Pee away," she said. "I'm not stopping you."

She left the room to make lunch.

It made her mad that he wouldn't talk to her. He *could* use that iPad to talk to her, but he wouldn't. He shut her out. She was the enemy. Because she wanted him to get better. Because, all right, she *pushed* him a little. (Doris pulled a pot out of the cupboard.) What a baby he was. (She whapped the pot on the stove.) What a child. (She ripped the tab off the box of squash soup and started glugging it into the pot).

She heard the toilet flush, heard Jonathan shuffle-whump his way back from the bathroom with the walker. She snuck a peek at him to make sure he was all right.

Oh, her grumpy old beloved.

There was a knock at the door. That was odd. They were very strict in the building about soliciting. No Greenpeace, no political canvassers, no Girl Scouts.

So who was knocking?

A kid. In a ball cap. With a dog. And a clipboard. And another kid. Possibly autistic. Hiding his eyes behind his hands. And a tiny grandma watching from down the hall.

"Hi. My name is Kid," said the first kid, looking at Doris's shoulder. Doris checked. Did she have a big glob of soup there? No. "I just moved into Apartment 1005. I'm doing a door-to-door survey of our building. Do you mind if I ask you a few questions?"

"I'm just getting lunch ready, and I — "

"Are you aware of a rumor that a goat lives on this building?"

"A goat?"

Jonathan shouted something.

"I'll be there in a minute," Doris called. "There's a kid at the door asking about goats."

"E ih oo um ih," said Jonathan.

Honestly, Doris thought. He said nothing when you wanted him to talk and shouted when you tried to talk to someone else.

"Some say mountain goat, some say billy goat."

"I don't understand. What are you asking me?"

"If you've ever seen a goat on or about the building."

"You have to be kidding," said Doris.

"E ih oo um ih," shouted Jonathan.

"Jonathan! I am talking to one of our neighbors! I will be right. There." She turned back to the child. "No. I haven't seen a goat."

The kid sighed and stowed her pencil. "Well, thank you for your time."

"O-ih!" came the moan.

"Coming, Jonathan," she said. "Please excuse my husband. He's had a stroke."

The little gang — kids, dog and grandma — turned away.

"How would a goat get on our building?" she asked herself as she checked on the soup.

4

Kenneth P. Gill — Kenneth to his friends — did not like hiking.

He liked Manhattan. He liked restaurants, concerts, theaters, crowds, concrete, all-night eateries, food delivery, movies, television, gyms and fashionable shoes.

He did not like being cold. He did not like being sweaty. He despised fleece. He stayed in shape by jogging on a treadmill while watching business news on the television. He showered immediately afterward.

Kenneth's father, on the other hand, had loved hiking. And biking. And mountain climbing. And canoeing. All self-propelled wilderness pursuits. Preferably for months at a time. Kenneth's father liked being cold and sweaty. Kenneth's father, in fact, had an affection for what he called "good, clean dirt." Also for bathing in glacial streams.

Kenneth's father had been a lawyer in Seattle, which is where Kenneth grew up. Kenneth's mother didn't mind the out of doors as long as there were doors nearby that led to a nice cozy indoors or, better yet, inn.

Throughout Kenneth's childhood, the family spent one week of summer vacation at a cabin on the Olympic Peninsula. Then Kenneth and his mother went back to the city or to Ashland to watch Shakespeare while his father went off on some expedition — kayaking in Alaska, climbing in British Columbia, that sort of thing.

Once a year, his father insisted they go on a father-son adventure.

Kenneth tried to like backpacking. No, that's not true. You can't even try to like something that makes your back a wall of sweat and makes you wear ugly shoes that give you blisters the first sixteen times you wear them and that forces you to "reconstitute" something that was once food but is now a mummy.

He liked the views. The views were nice. But he didn't like worrying about bears. He didn't like hearing mice run up the sides of the tent at night. He didn't like lying awake while a mosquito threw its voice so he slapped himself silly and never got the offending bug. He didn't like pooping over holes in the ground, dug and covered by himself with a small spade.

But he loved his father, who was wiry in body and tender in soul. So he went. And he pretended not to completely hate it. And when he was sixteen his father said, "This might be our last year to do this, Kenny." So he planned a backpacking trip through the Cascades into Canada. For a *week*.

Kenneth survived. His father was happy. It was kind of sad that his father was so happy about nice views and being together.

Kenneth's father always joked when they emerged from the bush about how they must smell all grungy. He liked to hang onto that smell. He liked the idea of other people smelling them, finding them pungent, while they themselves did not, because they were used to their own smells. His father wanted to get a meal at a diner and drive right home and shower there, but Kenneth insisted they stop at a motel for a shower and a proper bed.

In the shower, Kenneth tipped his head back under the glorious hot water rinsing out the shampoo and said to himself, "I never have to do this again." He smiled and soaped up his chest and sang.

The next summer he got a job working for his uncle at the Pacific Stock Exchange in San Francisco. Then he got a scholarship to university in New York and met his wife and there he stayed.

Every year, his father would ask at Christmas if Kenneth wanted to join whatever expedition he was planning for the coming summer. Kenneth said no to Denali, Baffin Island, Antarctica, Kamchatka, the Gobi Desert, Sakhalin Island, Mount Fuji, Nepal, the Andes, the Amazon, the Great Lakes, the Appalachian Trail, the West Coast Trail, the Columbia River, the Nahanni River, Tasmania, New Zealand, Florida swamp, Joshua Tree and the Sierra Madre.

And then his father died in his sleep. He was seventy-four. Not so old, really. Kenneth had thought he'd live till ninety.

The will asked Kenneth to scatter his ashes in the Cascades. That was his favorite expedition, the will said. It wasn't the longest or the hardest or the farthest away, but it was the best because it was with his son.

All of which is why Kenneth found himself, one foggy day in mid-June with a whiff of snow still in the air, hiking along a narrow trail between a rock wall and a glacial lake.

His father hadn't specified where, exactly, he wanted his ashes scattered. Kenneth sort of thought maybe the lake would do, though it was possible that high on one of the ridges might be a place he'd liked better. The ashes were in a ziplock bag, and he carried them in the pocket of his dad's fleece jacket for easy access.

Luckily it was a large pocket. The jacket hung to that side because the ashes were heavy, like a bag of sand.

On the drive up, the ashes had been on the passenger seat. Kenneth chatted to them.

"So you're what's left of Dad, huh? You don't seem much like him. He was much more, you know, fleshy. A little less ashen. Ha ha."

Kenneth talked to his father's ashes on and off the whole drive, and when he stepped out of the car at the trailhead, he cached the car keys the way his father always did so they wouldn't get lost on the trail, and tucked the heavy ash bag into his pocket.

"Well, off we go, Dad. How far? I could let you out here. Ha ha. Joke."

Truth is, Kenneth was lonelier than he'd realized. And sadder. His wife had left him. His goldfish had died. And it turned out he didn't have that many friends. It hadn't seemed that way before his wife left. She organized dinner parties and nights out with other couples and had been great company herself and it had seemed like they had plenty of friends.

His wife leaving him had really taken him by surprise. He had thought they were doing just fine, but she fell in love with somebody else.

He told his dad's ashes the whole story. How she decamped to Florida, where her new boyfriend had a sculpture studio on Key West and a fishing boat. How devastated he had been.

The ashes didn't talk back and at night Kenneth tucked them into his sleeping bag as he lay looking up at the stars.

His father had loved sleeping under the stars. If Kenneth breathed in a certain way and blurred his mind in a certain way, he could feel his father beside him, hands behind his head, mind fixed on the stars, saying, "There's one," each time a star fell. "The world is a beautiful place, my son."

"It has its sucky moments, too, Dad," Kenneth said.

"Now's not one of them, though, is it?"

"Well, except that you're dead. That's a little sucky."

They lay there for a time in silence, Kenneth and his imaginary father.

"Why do we think stars are beautiful?" Kenneth said. "I mean, we all agree they are, right? But why should we think that?"

"Just the way we are, I guess."

"If we weren't here, would the stars still be beautiful?"

Dew was settling on Kenneth's sleeping bag, making it clammy and uncomfortable. There was a rock under his shoulder blade if he shifted left and a root if he shifted right. His face was freezing where it stuck out of his father's super-duper extra-warm hooded sleeping bag. His nose began to drip.

"Isn't the cold air wonderful?" said Kenneth's dad.

"No," said Kenneth. His breath made clouds in the air.

"Aw, come on."

"You're not really here."

Something opened in Kenneth's chest, and he cried, missing his father. He felt alone. It felt like there *were* no people, that he was the last person, the only person. That it was up to him to see the beauty in everything because when he was gone, there would be no more beauty because there would be no human consciousness to see it.

He wondered if animals understood beauty. Maybe. But he sort of thought they were so deeply beautiful themselves that they could not see beauty. They could not stand outside themselves to see it.

He heard rustling — probably mice — and wished he'd put up the tent after all. He doubted he would sleep. His fingers on the baggie were sweaty.

He felt the self go out of him, walk out of his chest into the stars, so that the thing in the sleeping bag was some kind of shell, a him-shell.

And then he was conscious of waking.

It was foggy. Not a blanket fog but a fog that hung in patches. A cloud-walking fog. Kenneth made himself some oatmeal out of a packet, packed up and walked on.

"When will I know, Dad? When will I know it's time to scatter you?"

He felt funny. Something was happening to him. He wasn't as bothered by the regular discomforts.

"Is it better to be in water or on land?" he asked. "Do you want to be all in one place?"

What did it mean to scatter somebody's ashes? How did life come into being? How did it stop?

It was hard not to think that there had to be a continuous stream of life somewhere. You bobbed up in it when you were conceived, it carried you along for a while, and then it went somewhere else.

Kenneth couldn't picture heaven. Too static.

But a river. Or a thread. Something long and continuous and probably looping and poking through fabrics every now and then to an unknown side and coming back again. Something like that he could sort of see.

As he was traipsing along in the patchy fog with these thoughts, the path became less cushiony. Not earth and evergreen needles anymore, but pebble and stone over bedrock.

And here, on his right-hand side, was not a forest any longer but a rock wall a little more than arm's length away. And there, on his left, the rock fell away again another arm's length out. There was water below.

And then the fog lifted, and Kenneth saw the lake and its green sides curving up into mountains and at the far end a glacier calving and trees and snow and peaks and wisps of cloud.

He was on a narrow path alongside the lake. The cliff was steep on either side of him, the lake about two bus lengths below.

"Here," the baggie said to Kenneth.

"Here?" said Kenneth. He actually wanted to keep going. Even if this was the ash-emptying spot and he had, at this point in the trail, fulfilled his purpose.

He would honor his father by hiking the whole trail, going the whole distance, even though he didn't need to. Even though he emptied the ashes here, down this cliff, into the water.

He unzipped the ziplock. He looked into the bag.

"Ready?" he said.

He took a big breath, breathed it out. He put his palm under the bottom of the bag so its weight rested there. He pulled the edges of the bag down so it was almost inside out. And then he tossed the ashes the way he'd toss a ball to imitate a pop fly.

They didn't go up so high but they made a beautiful gray arc as they dropped. And they pocked against the cliff edge and plopped into the water.

He shook the bag, fully inside out now. The last few bits fell on the path at his feet. He crouched down and eyed them with affection as if they were a wild animal he'd hand-raised and was now releasing into the wilderness.

"Go. Go on. Go."

At the same time that Kenneth P. Gill was scattering his father's ashes in the Cascade Mountains, Jonathan and Doris were sailing. At last.

It had taken a lot of hard work to talk Jonathan into retiring, but Doris finally managed it when he was seventy-two. Now was the time for their great sailing adventure. Now, while they both still had their health. The plan was that they would sail leisurely down the Atlantic, explore the Caribbean, go through the Panama Canal, sail up the West Coast and then back again.

Every weekend for two years they worked to make sure their boat was shipshape, that they knew all the safety protocols and were experienced with big winds and weather. They took courses. They rehearsed falling overboard and rescuing each other in Long Island Sound.

It was hard work for a couple of seventy-year-olds. Their friends could not believe it, especially voluntarily going overboard in Long Island Sound. They were both healthy and limber. You might have guessed they were in their fifties rather than their seventies.

On board the boat, Doris loved having Jonathan all to herself. They played Scrabble. They read aloud to each other. They sang songs from their youth. They talked about their grown children.

The weather was good, except for one day of rain and low winds. The big storm they thought was going to hit missed them.

They never called it a second honeymoon, but that's what it felt like. A time all these years later when the world was made up of just the two of them.

They were about twenty miles out from Bermuda. Doris was at the helm.

It was one o'clock, a gorgeous day, a perfect wind.

Jonathan was fixing lunch. He'd been pleased with his shipboard culinary success. Pleased to have managed flatbread on the little galley stove, and to have got beansprouts started so they had fresh greens.

He was coming up the stairs from the cabin with a tray and an air of triumph. Doris could see the lightness in his step, hear his unconscious hum.

And then she saw him stop. Saw his left hand drop the tray. Saw him swing to the right. Saw him fall back down the hatch.

"Jonathan!" she cried.

She fixed the wheel to maintain their course and raced to the hatch. He was at the bottom of it, conscious, half-paralyzed.

Stroke? Heart attack? She knew right away it was one of the two. She felt his pulse. Fast but steady, she thought, though her own pulse was beating like a scared rabbit's. She checked his breathing. Ragged but steady. His pupils — the right one twice as large as the left.

Stroke.

"It's all right, Jojo," she said. "We're almost to Bermuda. I'll radio for help."

He said something she couldn't at first decipher. As she raced to the radio, she realized what it was.

"I love you, too," she shouted, and radioed for help.

A Bermudan coast-guard boat came out to get him. It was the longest four hours she could remember.

She docked, caught a cab to the hospital and held Jonathan's hand.

When he was strong enough, they flew back to New York, and Jonathan started rehab.

He hated it. He went on strike. He sat there, limp and angry and uncommunicative.

"If he's giving up, I'm giving up," Doris told her friend Charlotte.

But the truth was, Doris was not capable of giving up. And she knew that depression and mood and personality changes were part of stroke and stroke recovery. So she girded her loins and kept going, kept trying to be cheerful, kept talking to Jonathan.

One day he would come around. He had to.

People think that mountain goats never fall. The epitome of nimbleness and balance fall? Impossible.

But mountain goats live on mountains. And mountains are steep and mountains are high and gravity pulls downward.

So, yeah. Sometimes they fall.

But that's not what happened to the goat's mother. Not exactly.

The goat's mother jumped.

But before that, she gave birth. She was pregnant, tripping along the mountainside, when all of a sudden she thought, Oh. Ledge. I need a ledge. A ledge with a little bit of grass and a lot of safety from things that pounce.

So she found herself a ledge like that.

And then she thought, I am going to give birth.

And she did. Out came a little wet sac o' goat.

She licked it off. He was small and had a short little face and thin nostrils and, once licked, his fur began to fluff up. Already he could baa a little and butt his head against the air until he found what he wanted.

His mother's teat. Milk.

A mist floated over them. They rested and slept. Then the little goat, the kid, felt a funny urge to try out those spindly pegs attached to his body.

Oup. Oup. Oup-oup. There. Ooh. Whoa. They sure are wobbly. But fun. Hoo. Look! Look! If you go like this, you move forward! Or, wait. Go like this, you go back! You can go up, too! This is incredible. Wow.

Yes, it's called gamboling, said his mother's eyes. Stay away from the edge. Settle down.

Settle down? Are you kidding? This is incredible. This is the best feeling in the —

No, wait. Milk. Milk is the best feeling. This is the second-best feeling in the — Oof. Well, how about that? You can't really kick with all four of these things at once, can you? Well, live and learn.

Eventually he did settle down. But, boy! Kicking and jumping and spinning around was incredibly excellent!

They hung out on their grassy ledge for a week or so. The ledge was about two mothers wide and four mothers long and while the kid gamboled, the mother munched.

Soon enough, there was no grass left and the kid was strong enough and sure enough to follow the ledge out.

It was a day of patchy fog. Which suddenly cleared. Which allowed a golden eagle a view of the week-old kid following its mother. On a ledge. A hundred feet above a forty-year-old man throwing some kind of gray pebble-like stuff in the air.

The eagle dove. The mother goat caught movement in her eye and turned her head. More movement. Up there.

The eagle swung its talons forward. The mother goat put her head down and leapt at the eagle.

Butt. She connected. The talons closed not on kid flesh but goat hair.

Kenneth P. Gill stood up after watching his father's ashes fall to the lake below, brushing off his hands.

An eagle cried. He looked up. Two white objects plummeted toward him, a big one and a small one.

Goats. There were goats falling through the air. The little one was coming right to him. All he had to do was — whump! — stick out his arms and — oof — catch it.

Kenneth bent his knees to cushion the goat's landing, slowed the goat's fall with his arms.

Its heart was beating madly — he could feel that right away — and it struggled, squirming.

And then its eyes looked into his and it calmed and now he could feel his own heart beating fast.

"Dad?" said Kenneth.

The goat looked at him. Those eyes. They were Dad's eyes.

The stream of life. It was some kind of freakish miracle. Or maybe not freakish at all. Maybe not even a miracle.

Maybe, thought Kenneth P. Gill, it was a quite ordinary occurrence.

As soon as Kenneth put the goat down, the kid trotted over to his mother and nosed at her. Kenneth did not know that the mother goat had saved her kid from becoming an eagle's breakfast. He thought she had committed a sort of goat suicide in order to deliver her son, the reincarnation of his father, into his arms.

He thanked her.

The goat raised his head, bleated, looked over at Kenneth, then trotted straight toward him. He butted Kenneth's shin.

Kenneth thought about continuing on the trail. He wondered about living in the wilderness with his goat-father. But the baby goat kept butting his legs. He wanted milk and wasn't eating anything else.

Kenneth made up some milk from powder, but that clearly didn't cut it as far as the goat was concerned.

He was going to have to get some goat's milk.

He didn't know that mountain goats are technically not goats at all but a species of antelope. And when his own food was gone, what was he going to do? He did not know how to forage for wild food. He certainly wouldn't be able to kill anything in order to eat it.

Kenneth decided he had to take his father, in goat form, home. He would make up for all the time he had lost, all the trips he had refused to go on.

The airline, though, would ask questions. There was probably a law about transporting wild animals. You probably needed a certificate.

So Kenneth decided that he and the goat would take a road trip across America.

In the car, they bonded, Kenneth thought. Kenneth talked while the goat leapt from front seat to back, one side of the car to the other until he tired and curled up to sleep. At night, in motel rooms, after drinking five or six baby bottles of goat's milk Kenneth had picked up at a grocery store and pinballing around the room, the goat fell asleep snugged up against Kenneth.

There were mishaps. One time, when Kenneth was driving with his window open, the goat leapt onto

Kenneth's lap and would have jumped right out the window if Kenneth hadn't blocked him with his arm.

"Dad, I know you're full of verve," Kenneth said. "But you mustn't do that. We're lucky I didn't drive off the road! I'm sorry for all the times I said, 'Are we there yet,' okay?"

Another time, at a gas station in Illinois, someone filling up at the next pump saw the goat bouncing around the car and then putting his little hooves on the window.

"What kind of animal is that? Looks like a … mountain goat."

"Good eye," said Kenneth — smoothly, he thought. "It is a mountain goat. It was orphaned. In the mountains. I'm transporting it to the Central Park Zoo." He shivered inwardly with the lie.

Pretend it's true, he told himself. It's almost true. La la la. Not strange at all I'm transporting a mountain goat in a rental sedan. La la la.

"Wow," said the guy, replacing the nozzle and shutting the gas cap, snapping the cover shut. "Well, have a nice day."

Phew.

"That was a close call, Dad," Kenneth said as they pulled out onto the highway again.

As they entered the city, Kenneth's plan seemed less and less realistic. But just then the goat looked up from where he was curled on the passenger seat, and there was no doubt at all.

They were his father's eyes, and they were saying, "I love you, Kenneth. Thank you."

At last they made it to Manhattan and to Kenneth's building. A small, effortless ruse ("Julio, can you get my backpack from the curb there? I'll be back down for it in a minute") distracted the doorman as Kenneth wrapped the goat in his Gore-Tex jacket and they were in.

As soon as they got in the door of his apartment and Kenneth set his father down and his little hooves biffed the floor, Kenneth knew his downstairs neighbor would not take well to the new arrival. Kenneth threw all his towels on the floor, all his bedding. He ran down to get his backpack from Julio, came back up and covered as much floor as he possibly could.

He realized he needed something to eat. He could order in, but what could he order in for the goat?

The goat liked to jump on the coffee table and from the coffee table to the end table and from the end table to the dining-room table and from the dining-room table to the buffet, from the buffet to the windowsill to the dining-room table to the kitchen counter.

Now that the floor was strewn with soft things, he was not going to put hooves to it.

Then he started to eat Kenneth's shirts.

"Dad," said Kenneth. "I know you're playful and all, but could you do me a favor and lie low for a while?"

Goat poo was easy to handle. Neat little turds easily picked up and flushed. Not that he didn't step in a few first. Goat pee was trickier. He tried paper training his dad, but had limited success. He ended up washing a lot of towels.

The next day, Kenneth did his laundry, cleaned out his fridge, bought groceries, including almost a hundred dollars' worth of goat's milk, and wondered how he was going to give his dad enough exercise. Maybe a belt would work as a combined collar and leash? He tried, but Dad was having none of it. There was no way he was letting Kenneth put anything over his head or around his neck.

"I know you're a free spirit, Dad, but please. Give me a break here."

Then again, if he did manage to get some sort of leash on the goat, what was he going to do? Take him for a walk? Down the elevator and through the lobby where everyone could see? Kenneth was relatively certain goats were not on the list of the building's allowable pets.

The day after that, Kenneth had to go to work.

"Now don't get into trouble," he said to his father, shaking his finger at him.

He left him a bin full of grass clippings he'd thieved from the park. On the way home, he picked up more goat's milk.

•

One July night, Kenneth woke at three in the morning in a room so hot he thought for a second he was in a sauna. An oven. A kiln. It was unbearable. He had to open a window. He had to open all the windows.

He fell back into bed. A light *duth-duth* sound registered in his ear.

Like mountain goat hooves on a windowsill.

He sat up just in time to see the goat disappear from view.

"Daaaad!" he shouted and raced to the window.

There was a ledge just below the window. The goat was on this, but it seemed like he was on nothing at all, walking on air. It would take so little, such a small misstep, and the reincarnation of Kenneth P. Gill's father would fall to a second death.

"Dad," Kenneth hissed out the window. "Come back here." The goat continued along the ledge.

Kenneth ran to the fridge and with shaking hands filled a bottle with goat's milk. He ran back to the window.

"I've got your milkums here! Come and get it."

But the goat took no notice.

He jumped. Kenneth covered his eyes.

Then he heard a landing and opened his eyes. The goat was on the ledge of the window of the next apartment.

What would his father be born as next? He hadn't had very long as a goat. What could he have learned in such a short incarnation? It was beyond the powers of Kenneth P. Gill to know or understand. He accepted that.

He accepted all.

The loss of his father, his wife, his dreams, his comfort.

He left the window open, the bucket of grass on the floor just inside.

What a strange mountain he found himself on but how blessed the open air. He had been fooled by the warm tree-ish thing. It had given him milk but it had kept him in a cave. Now he could leap up and up and, oh. He was at the top. No, wait, a leap down, a traverse, a zigzag leap up.

Now he was at the top. There, down in the valley, was all the food a goat needed. Tomorrow he would go to the valley and feed. Tonight he would sleep here, on the highest point, curled under an outcrop, safe from the Dangers Above.

Safe-ish. You were never truly safe.

In the morning, he stood again, looking out toward the glorious valley.

But wait. There, just there on the wide ledge below him was a stand of trees. He would eat there first.

So it went each day. The goat woke, stretched, tried to gambol a little for old time's sake, stood majestically looking out over the valley, felt a wave of melancholy at its proximity and all the dangers that lay between him and it, and then at last was lured by the fresh food right in front of him. He would leap down to Joff's patio, nibble what cedars he could reach, blink at the friendly wolfish animal that lived on the other side of the glass, butt the glass door ("What was that, Michigan? A ten-pound pigeon? What the heck?"), and be off on his rounds to see what he could scrounge. A bucket of hay began appearing on the ledge outside the cave he had escaped from.

He stayed away at first, but as he grew hungrier, his danger gauge shifted. He could nab the hay and leap away at any danger. Definitely.

Some mornings, the melancholy was right there when he awoke, and he didn't get up at all. What was the point?

But then the wolfish animal would come out and look up at him, inviting him to come down, and he would not be able to help himself. He would hop down and gambol with it a little. ("Michigan, quit chasing pigeons! I'm trying to sleep here!")

Maybe today he would try to get to the green. And he would think about it all day while touring the ledges and nibbling up what few leaves he could find. Evening would come and he would start, lightly, down the clangy cliff that turned back on itself.

And then something would stop him. Maybe it was the tree-ish creatures on the clangy cliff bringing small fires to their mouths. Maybe it was the idea of getting back up after he'd gone down.

That last jump was a doozy.

5

Kenneth P. Gill was listening to opera and Swiffering his already clean floor when something startling happened.

Someone knocked on his door.

They'd come to get him.

They'd found out about the goat.

What should he do? Answer it?

No. He wasn't home. Nope. Nobody home. Just some opera playing. La la la.

Oh, no. Opera playing! They would *know* he was home.

Ah, but if it was really loud, how could he hear a knock? He turned it up.

"Nessun dor-maaaaa," he sang, then dropped an octave, "Nessun dorrrrmaaaaa. La la la la la la la-la ..."

Another tiny, distant knock.

He waited a few minutes, then went to the door and looked through the peephole.

There was the kid who was looking after Cat, Cat herself, and another kid, a thin little fellow with big eyes and floppy dark hair. Reminded him of himself as a kid. And a tiny older woman.

Huh. Maybe they were selling something?

Well, too bad. He was too wrapped up in his music to hear them. He raced away from the door so his voice would sound from a distance. "La la la la splenderà."

What did they want?

His guinea pigs! Maybe they wanted to see Wallace and Pita. Children liked guinea pigs. What had happened to Wallace and Pita? They, uh, caught a sudden disease and died. And …

Another knock! Augh! And … he'd got rid of their cage. Because it gave him too much pain to see it after their untimely deaths …

Knock!

He pinched his eyes shut. Please go away. Please go away. He opened one eye.

He checked the peephole. Ah. He felt his shoulders drop. Empty hallway.

Kenneth leaned his back against the door with his hand to his chest, feeling his heart gradually slow.

At 6:47 a.m., Jonathan opened his left eye. His right eye reluctantly followed. He smelled coffee.

Doris was up. She'd be in soon. He tossed off the covers and began his exercises. He drew his left knee to his chest. He tried to do the same with his right. It would not cooperate.

He closed his eyes and visualized the leg moving, as the physiotherapist had suggested.

He opened his eyes.

Yes! It worked. It was moving.

He heard Doris's sigh. The newspaper whispering closed. Herself standing from her chair. Coming in. He hurried to get his legs back in place, to pull up the covers and pretend to be just waking.

Her sigh had made him unaccountably sad.

"Good morning," she sang, as usual. She smiled. She was chipper. But it was put on. She was faking it. There was sadness behind her eyes.

She didn't *like* bullying him.

"Ud or," he said.

Her eyes softened and brightened. He had answered her! Instead of grumping, he had attempted a two-word sentence!

"Let's get these limbs moving!" she said, whipping off the bedcovers.

He feigned the usual reluctance. But it felt good to have her move his leg up and down, to support the foot as he bent his knee. Oh, it was so much easier than doing it by himself. He wasn't going to let her think he'd gone soft, mind. But he let her do it. What harm would it do?

He wanted to talk to the goat kid. Not the goat kid. The kid who had asked about the goat. Apartment 1005.

Over the course of a week, Kid and Will and Cat, with Dr. Lomp lurking in the background, canvassed five of eleven floors.

No one had seen the goat.

Kid had knocked on fifty-four doors. Twenty-three of them had been answered. Her eyes had fixed on many shoulders — old ones in suit jackets with little flakes of dandruff, round ones in African prints draped in dreadlocks, bare ones in cut-off T-shirts. And then on many earlobes — long and droopy, studded with diamonds, hooped with gold earrings.

Kid did not like knocking on doors any better at the end of five floors than she had at the beginning. But she was better at saying what she wanted to say. The whole thing genuinely got easier, even with the people who were super annoyed to have to come to the door and who thought Kid and Will were obnoxious children playing a joke like that one where you ask people if their refrigerator is running and then tell them they had better go catch it.

At first the door slammers made her cheeks hot and her throat tight. Now she just turned to Will and shrugged and went on to the next door.

It would be nice when they could say they had canvassed the whole building. Kid's enthusiasm for the project was waning, but she didn't want to give up without as full a data set as possible.

Today they were on the seventh floor. They'd knocked on seven doors and had five friendly people tell them no, they hadn't seen the goat.

Kid knocked on the eighth door and said, "Hi, we're doing a survey of the building to find out if anyone has seen a mountain goat rumored to live here" before she even realized she was *looking into a stranger's eyes*. Sea-green eyes in a brown face. Warm and kind.

"How very interesting," the man said. "And how resourceful of you to survey the building. Have you had any luck?"

"Not yet," said Kid, trying not to marvel that she was chatting with a stranger.

"I wish I had seen a goat," he said. "But I'm afraid I'll have to add to your stock of no's."

He wished them luck and they packed it in for the day.

Kid noticed in the elevator that there was a P button, which she presumed was for Penthouse.

Maybe, Kid thought, the person in the penthouse had seen the goat.

Back in the apartment, Bobby and Dr. Lomp played Scrabble in the living room while Will and Kid ate blueberry yoghurt at the dining-room table.

"The pie in the ghenthouse has to have seen the goat, right?" Kid said to Will. "I mean, if it lives on the building, and nobody sees it, then it must be on the roof, right?"

"And the renthouse is on the poof," said Will. "Ergo, the lote gives on the roof. Let's go."

"We're going to peck the chenthouse," said Will to the grown-ups.

Dr. Lomp rearranged her letters. "Take Cat," she said.

Will and Kid exchanged glances. She was letting them go on their own?

"Okay," said Will.

When they were in the hall and the door was closed behind them, Will jumped into the air. He jumped all the way to the elevator.

When he got in he put his hand on his chest and said, "Hoo, I feel a little funny."

"Should we go back?"

"No. I'm okay." He put his hand on Cat's head. Kid pressed the P button. The elevator door closed.

"Wow. I've read about this," said Will. "I feel like Huck Finn. Kids in books never have adults around."

"At home, me and Luna and Charlie do things on our own all the time."

"Lucky."

"I wonder if the elevator door opens right into his apartment." Kid had seen this on TV.

It didn't. It opened into a small hallway. The door to the penthouse apartment was straight ahead. To the left and to the right were exits — doors that opened by pressing on a bar like in a school.

They knocked on the penthouse door.

No answer. They knocked again.

"He must be out."

"Let's go check the roof," said Kid.

"Doh nan coo."

"Will, could you *some*times talk in regular talk so a person can understand you?"

"No can do." Will's eyes were closed.

"It's right here. The door's right here. We're in the middle of the building. We can't fall off even if we try. Plus, I'm sure there's like, a wall or a railing or something at the edge of the building. Look, I'll just peek out."

Will covered his eyes.

Kid opened the door. She and Cat stepped through. A wind blew in. All she could see was a sort of outdoor corridor, pebbles on tar and a vent. The corridor came to a T a little farther on and straight ahead across the T was a wall about chest height to keep you from falling over the edge of the building.

Her heart beat hard.

She needed something to prop the door open.

"Will, can you — "

"No," he said.

She took off her shoe and wedged it in the door. The pebbles hurt her foot. Cat trotted out ahead of her and around the corner to the left. Cat would know if there was a goat on the roof, right?

Oh, no. What if Cat chased the goat on the roof? What would happen then? A goat was not even vaguely rat-like. But the fact was, Cat liked to chase wildlife.

Kid followed at a trot, hop-limping on her unshod foot. The path turned again and came to a dead end. If you looked over the edge you'd see the little court-yard where the dumpster was. Cat was already turning back the way they'd come. Now she headed past the corridor they'd emerged from and continued to the end of the building that faced Central Park.

Wind caught the brim of Kid's cap. She had to clap a hand on to keep it from flying off. It felt as if the wind could lift her right up into the sky.

A rush of fear blew through her. She felt bad for being annoyed with Will. She kept on, though, to the wall at the end and looked out over Central Park.

It was huge. Her eyes watered in the wind. Pigeons wheeled in the sky. She looked for the falcon but didn't see it. To the right, a fence and a row of sick-looking cedars blocked off what seemed like the penthouse deck.

No goat.

She retraced her steps.

Her shoe was gone. The door was shut. What the heck?

She knocked, hoping Will had not abandoned her.

He hadn't. Will opened the door with his eyes closed and his face screwed up.

"Why did you leave the door open?" he asked. "It was awful. I nearly threw up. I had to close it."

"You closed it? Do you hear that? You closed it. And you opened it again! That's amazing."

"Do not do that again." After a minute, he asked, "Did you see anything?"

"No."

"Let's go back down. Please." It was like Will was holding his breath. Kid pressed the Down button beside the elevator. He breathed out again once they were safely inside.

Kid wondered why Will wasn't bothered by elevators. Why windows and rooftop doors but not elevators?

She didn't want to ask in case asking made him afraid of elevators, too.

Back in the apartment, the grown-ups asked how it went.

"He wasn't there," said Will casually, as if they'd just gone up, knocked on the door and come back down.

Kid waited for them to ask what had taken so long. But they did not ask.

After two weeks of daily visits to Washington Square with no sight or tell of Mara, Joff came to a sad conclusion.

Mara was a tourist. She had come to New York, she had left New York, never to return.

He had met her once, he bravely told himself. That was enough.

Maybe he could use that somehow in his novel. A woman who inspires the hero the whole way through the book, and who he meets in the end.

Yeah. That's what he would do. He would stay home and write. He would not go out.

Twenty minutes passed. He wrote nothing. His legs were twitchy. He got up and jogged on the spot for a while.

Maybe he should get a treadmill. He'd read about writers who wrote while on a treadmill.

The room felt stuffy. He opened the sliding glass door and stepped out onto the deck. Pigeons flapped. Sirens called. He could hear the occasional shout from the street below. Someone hollering, "Taxi!" Someone shouting to someone across the street about deliveries.

"My feet feel like skating, Michigan," he said. "Let's go. Not to Washington Square, though. Not today. Today, let's just meander."

And so Joff meandered out the front door ("Thanks, Julio!") across the street and into the park ("Man, nature smells good") and meandered down Fifth Avenue ("Watch out, buckaroo!").

Just meandering, you know, not heading any particular direction until …

There he was. Back at Washington Square.

"Joffey's back! Yo, Joffey."

"Hey, Chili, you — "

"Naw, we ain't seen her today neither. You gon play? Two minutes, I'll beat you in two minutes. Come on. Sit down. Let's play."

6

On Wednesdays, Doris volunteered for an adult literacy program at the Y. She left Jonathan with soup, a glass of water and a glass of Scotch, the phone with her cell number on speed dial, and the crossword. His walker was always parked within reach. It had a bag on it so he could carry things.

Now he put his little tablet in there in case he had trouble with pencil and paper, which were in his breast pocket. He drew the walker to him, locked the wheels and stood up. He held up his left foot and did the circular exercises. Then the same with his right. He took the walker in hand, unlocked it and headed for the door.

Phew. Not easy. But he was doing it. He was moving. Under his own steam. Both legs. The easy left and the tricky right. His arms felt shaky.

Okay. Now he had to maneuver around the idiotic

electric scooter Doris had got him that he refused to demean himself with. He bashed it with the walker for good measure while skirting it.

Now he was at the elevator.

What? He had to let go of the walker to push the button? Of course he did. How silly not to think of that.

Okay, right arm. You're on. Go! Lift, point, there. You can do it, you can do it. Up a little, that's it. There!

When the elevator dinged open he realized how short the time available to enter an elevator was. You had to be moving the second it opened.

He couldn't even get the walker in the door before it closed.

Damn. Now he had to push the button again. There.

Why wasn't the door opening?

The elevator clunked.

Oh. Because someone had called it to another floor. He'd have to wait. And be ready.

He watched the lights climb the numbers above the elevator.

Six, seven, eight, nine … go! He pushed off. Right foot. Your turn. Come on. You can do it. He visualized walking easily.

Ding!

There's the door. Now's the time. Go. Go. Come on, legs, arms. Move it, move it —

Darn!

Jonathan tried to get on the elevator three more times. Each time the door closed on him before he could jam the walker in front of the rubber bumper.

By the fourth time, he was starting to feel a little shaky.

And then the door opened, and Mrs. Grbzc stood there.

"Jonathan!" she said. "How wonderful to see you on your feet, sallying forth. Let me hold the door for you."

Jonathan shook his head, turned his walker back toward his apartment. He made a gesture as if to show that all he was doing was walking up and down the halls for rehab. And then he walked up and down the halls for rehab.

He'd make it onto that elevator next time.

It took four minutes just to get his apartment door open and another four to make it past the … hmmmm … scooter.

The door flew open. Lisa stood in the doorway.

"Aaagh! Previews start in three days!"

"Aroo," said Cat. She hopped off the couch and stood at Lisa's knee, wagging her tail.

"We are sunker than sunk," cried Lisa. "We're a wreck. We are on the ocean floor. Divers are swimming through us looking for relics."

Kid closed the door behind Lisa. Bob took Lisa by the shoulders and led her into the living room. He sat her down. Cat leapt up and put a paw on her leg.

Lisa put her head in her hands.

"The star doesn't know her lines. The juggling number is a disaster. The soccer balls are flying everywhere. I mean, into the audience! It's dangerous. It's horrible." She made little whimpering noises.

Kid brought a soda water with lime, just the way Lisa liked it. Bobby rubbed her back.

"Sh," said Bobby. "It'll be okay. It'll be fine."

"It won't, it won't, it won't," Lisa said.

"Listen. Lisa. You are not a toddler. You can handle this."

"It was a bad idea."

Kid put on soothing classical piano music at low volume.

"Turn that off," said Lisa. Kid turned it off.

"*Soccer Mom*. It's not sexy. It's not based on a movie or a TV show."

"You've got a star."

"Our star needs auto-tune and a personal line prompter."

"She's still a star."

"She's not a young star. It's a musical about middle-aged women! Whose terrible idea was that? Oh, that's right, mine."

"Middle-aged women buy theater tickets for their families," said Bobby.

"Middle-aged women buy theater tickets for their families to see shows based on Disney movies or superheroes."

"Girls' night out? Ever hear of that?"

"Gay men are totally not going to want to see this."

"It's got a gay kid in it!"

"Conservatives will picket!"

At last they managed to get her to go for a run, come home and take a bath, and play Uno with them. She played ruthlessly and still lost. She dropped her head to the table.

"It's an omen. My life is over."

"Mom," said Kid. "Go to bed."

"Are you kidding? You think I can sleep?"

She was still up watching Mary Tyler Moore DVDs when Kid went to bed.

Kid *had* to find that goat. Soon.

This time Jonathan took the scooter. Each time Doris had gone out in the past week, he'd practiced. First he had to get himself to the scooter with the walker. Then he had to lower his butt onto the seat and lift his feet onto the base.

Turning it on was easy enough. But the throttle! Whew! Talk about hair-trigger.

His first time, he bashed into the door. Now he turned the handle — gently, gently, there — to the door. Then turn the doorhandle. Gently, gently back up. Gently, gently — uh-oh — bam! Damn. Back up, opening the door a little more. Gently, gently through the door, pull it shut. Ah.

Down the hall to the elevator. Press the button. Wait. Watch numbers. Ready. Ding. Throttle. Whoa. Too much. Ack. Bash.

But he was in! He was in the elevator! Yes, ladies and gentlemen! Jonathan Fenniford was in the elevator. Now he just had to get turned around — bash — a little three-point turn — bash — and press the button for the tenth floor.

Success! The elevator rose.

The doors opened. He sailed off. He knocked at the door of 1005.

I'm in a scooter! he suddenly thought as the door opened. Oh, what life has brought me to.

A man stood there. With a dog Jonathan vaguely remembered seeing before. Different man than usual, though.

"Hi," said the man.

"O," said Jonathan. Damn. He had foreseen nothing. None of the difficulty of getting up here and of making himself understood.

Wait. Yes, he had. His little tablet was with him. But how to get it out?

"Are you all right?" the man asked. "Do you need help?"

Jonathan nodded to the first, then realized this might be construed as a reply to the second question. He grumped and reached for the tablet in the scooter's basket.

He could not reach it. Wait, yes, he could. But he could not grasp it. His hand did not want to work.

"This? You're reaching for this?" the man said, handing him the tablet. Jonathan nodded.

Now the kid came and stood at the door.

"Who is it, Bobby?"

"O," Jonathan said. He turned on the little computer and began to type his message.

"Hello," said the kid.

R U looking for a goat? he typed and showed to the kid.

"Yes. I am looking for a goat," she said in amazement.

There was another kid and a tiny woman also now crowding the doorway.

I saw it, Jonathan typed. *I see it often. It eats my wife's wheatgrass.*

The boy said, "You'll have seven gears of lewd yuck then. I mean, seven years of good luck."

Jonathan to the kid: *Do I look like luck is on my side?*

The kid shrugged. "You're alive," he said.

"You've seen the goat?" said the man. "The goat the kids have been looking for? I thought it was an urban myth."

No myth, typed Jonathan. *There's a goat. I think it lives on the roof.*

"Ha ha ha." The boy danced, kicking his feet out.

"Woo!" shouted the other. "Let's go." She headed for the elevator. The dancing kid followed, hopping with excitement. The dog pranced along with them.

"Wait," called the dad. "Wait for us." Then he looked at Jonathan.

Jonathan waved at them. Go, go. But still they hesitated.

Go, he gestured again.

"I will stay here with the gentleman," said the tiny woman. "You go."

They hesitated yet again as if they could not quite believe this.

Go, go, he waved.

"Yes, go," she repeated.

"Come on!" They were happy. Gleeful.

"So there is a goat. I was not certain," said the small woman to Jonathan. "I am Zinta Lomp." She opened the door. "Please come in."

He scooted into the hall, made a very nice tight turn — if he did say so himself — into the living room.

Jonathan Fenniford, wrote Jonathan.

"You've had a stroke."

"Yeh," said Jonathan. "Hard to 'peak."

"Coffee?" she said.

The goat curled in the corner of Joff's deck between two cedars. His stomach hurt. His head hurt. His joints hurt. He could not sleep and he could not wake up. He could not remember gamboling. He was in a sort of slow dream.

The waggy thing came and nudged him.

He sensed something different, an unfamiliar sound. He should really, he should really …

No. Never mind. His eyes were heavy. His head was heavy. How had he ever been able to lift it? It was like a stone.

Will was jumping up and down. Kid poked the elevator button. The light above it said it was at the lobby.

"Want to take the stairs?" said Bobby.

They headed for the stairs. Cat clattered ahead of them. Will and Kid leaped two stairs at a time. Bobby jogged behind them.

"What's the rush?" he said. "It's not going anywhere."

But there was a goat up there. A goat! On their building.

If the goat existed, then the goat's good luck existed, too.

It was only three floors, six flights of stairs. Cat waited at the top, where there was a door. Did it open onto the open roof or into the elevator room? Will didn't say anything, but he let Kid move ahead. She quick-looked at him before opening it.

They both let out their breath. Just the elevator lobby. And there. The door to the outside, the one she'd gone out before.

Was Will going to go through? He was. He was beside her. They were both pressing the bar that opened the door. They were opening it.

"Gets lo," he said.

They stepped out into the light of the late afternoon and onto the pebbled surface of the roof. Cat put her nose down and turned left toward the back of the building, the part over the alley. With the wall running around it, the roof felt perfectly safe, but it was still a roof.

"Find something to stop the door with, Dad," shouted Kid.

There was an electrical shed, a few vents, a big cylindrical thing, pipes sticking up. Cat sniffed back and forth, back and forth. She seemed to catch a scent and followed it to the iron ladder that went up and over the guard wall to the fire escape on the alley side.

She stopped, tipped her nose up into the air and sniffed some more, cocked her head a little, looked puzzled. Then she turned around and went back the way they'd come, past the door.

"She's a bull terrier, not a bloodhound," said Bobby, turning around and following her. He had one stockinged foot. Like Kid before him, he had stopped the door with his shoe.

Kid and Will ran past him. Kid wanted to ask Will how he was doing, but she didn't want to call attention to the fact that he was running around on a roof.

It was not a tall building. By Manhattan standards it was short. But twelve stories was enough to have you up pretty high. The wind was stronger than down below. The pigeons when they flapped were closer. It smelled of hot tar and dust and warm brick. They came to a fence with cedars behind it — the penthouse deck.

"It's not here," said Will. His eyes changed. He looked like he was going to pass out. And then he did. Fell right to the gravel at Kid's feet.

"Aroooo," said Cat. "Aroooo."

Kid and Bobby knelt by Will, taking his hand. He opened his eyes. Blinked. Looked not bad, all things considered. Looked like he'd be fine.

Cat licked his face.

"It's going nowhere," Joff said to his sister in Ann Arbor over Skype. She'd asked how his novel was going. "I'm going crazy because I keep thinking about this woman I met playing chess. I only met her once and I think I'm in love. Is that possible? Plus, I've been hearing this noise. It's really distracting. I called the building manager to see if they were doing any work on the roof, but no, apparently not. I don't know what it is."

"Whoa, Joffey, wait, back up. You met a woman playing chess?"

"Down at Washington Square. Mara. She had this beautiful round voice and she was funny and she said 'buckaroo' and I can't stop thinking about her. Every day since I met her I've gone back to see if she's there and she never is, so she was probably a tourist and I'm probably never going to see her again and it's kind of breaking my heart."

A faint *Aroooo* sounded behind Joff's words.

"What's that?" said Laura.

"It's kind of breaking my — "

"No, not that — "

The *Arooo* sounded again.

"That. Is that Michigan?"

"No, Michigan's right here." Joff turned his ear. There was definitely a dog howling nearby, a sort of a woe-is-me howl.

"Turn on the video," said Joff's sister.

"Why didn't I think of that?"

"Because you're blind."

Sisters. "Thanks. Okay. Here we go." Joff turned on the camera.

"Hi, Michigan," said his sister.

Michigan wagged his tail.

Joff picked up his laptop and turned it outward as he walked out to the deck. The howling continued intermittently and now they could hear voices, too.

"I can hear people but I can't see them," said his sister.

"Really," said Joff. "How strange. What's that like?"

"Shut up. Wait, what's that white lump under the tree there?"

"Hello?" Joff said to the voices. "Is something wrong?"

"Uh, hi," came a man's voice from the other side of the fence. "We were just — "

"It looks like a dog bed," said Joff's sister. "That's lifting its head."

"What?"

"It's getting up. It's not a dog bed. It's a — "

"Goat!" said a voice from the other side of the fence. "It's the goat. Will! We found the goat!"

"They're right. It's a goat. A mountain goat."

Joff heard the *flep-flep flep-flep* of the goat's hooves on the deck.

"That's it! That's the sound!"

"Wow. Look at it go. Did you see that?"

"Obviously, Laura, I did not see that."

"It just jumped, like, boop boop boop boop, deck table fence roof. Amazing!"

"There it goes," came the voices on the other side of the fence.

And then their footsteps running after it.

Weak though he was, the goat's body acted instantaneously.

He sensed danger.

He leapt.

Up.

Over.

Along.

Up.

Over.

Down.

Down the clangy cliff.

Down past the bucket ledge.

Down the clangy cliff! Unbelievable! Down.

The final jump. Cliff face, hoof it, purposeless ledge.

Down! He was down! All the way down! He was close to the glorious smell.

Close-ish.

There it was! Cantering along the wall-top like a raggedy mop on four legs.

"There it goes," said Will.

They took off after it. Holy, it was fast. Did it ever make running twelve stories above the pavement with three inches to spare look easy.

"Ow" (crunch), "ow" (crunch), went Bobby each time his socked foot hit the pebbles. His shoe was still in the door they were running past.

"Hello?" said Joff, poking his head out the door. Michigan's head poked out, too.

"It's heading for the fire escape," called Bobby.

So it was. It was ten feet from the iron ladder that went up and over the safety wall.

And then it was in the air. And then it was gone.

Kid's heart mimicked it, a millisecond behind. It leapt, it hung in the air …

Fwed-fwed, fwed-fwed. It landed. Phew.

"It's gone down the fire escape," said Will. "Let's go."

Kid couldn't believe it. Will was already climbing the ladder that took you over the wall and onto the fire escape. For the second time in less than a minute, she felt like she was watching a cartoon character who has run off a cliff but doesn't know it yet.

She took a deep breath and followed. Bobby picked up Cat and came next.

"I'm going to see what's going on," said Joff.

"Take me with you," said Laura.

Joff and Michigan (and Laura) jogged to the foyer. The door to the rooftop was propped open. Joff could hear someone going *Ow, ow, ow,* as well as running footsteps.

"Hello?" he called.

"It's heading for the fire escape," shouted a child's voice.

"I can't see," said Laura. "Turn me around."

Joff turned the computer around and followed the sound of the footsteps. Now there was a light sound. The goat landing on the fire-escape landing. Strains of opera floating up from an apartment below them.

"I can't see the goat anymore," said Laura. "The kids are following it. There's a guy picking up a white dog and carrying it over the fire escape."

What wacky goings-on on his rooftop!

"Hold me up!" said Laura. They were at the wall now, at the fire escape. The opera was louder and dramatic.

"I don't want to drop you," said Joff.

"Come on," said Laura. "Let's go."

"What?"

"Come on, up and over, they're getting away."

The music hit an incredible peak, a soaring moment, a long-held note. It tugged at something in him.

"Joff!" shouted his sister.

Right. They were following a goat. And two kids and a man and a dog named Cat.

"Laura, think for a second. I can't go over the wall *and* carry you. And what about Michigan?"

"But, Joff …"

"Look down, Laura. Can you see them?" Joff was dimly aware of the music ending, of speaking voices taking its place.

"All I can see is a brick wall."

Joff shifted the angle of the laptop. "Now?"

"The alley."

"Now?"

"I can't see, the people are in the — Oh, wait. The goat's down! It's in the alley, it's …"

But Joff wasn't listening to his sister anymore. He was listening to the radio. To the interview. To the voice. Round. Deep, like a well or a quarry.

Mara wasn't a tourist. She was an opera singer. At the Met. All this week.

Without thinking, he closed his laptop. His sister's voice disappeared. He leaned on the wall and listened to Mara.

Mara, Mara, Mara.

Man, that goat was fast. It was down each flight of the fire escape in one leap.

Will was only a little ahead of Kid now. Cat was in between them. Bobby was behind.

As they passed the second-from-top floor, a man stuck his head out the window.

"Dad?" he called. His eyes were on the goat. He climbed out the window onto the fire escape and joined the chase.

Now the goat was on the lowest landing of the fire escape, the one that was almost a full-story drop to the ground. There was a ladder on the wall that would descend if you put your weight on it, but the goat did not know that.

It hesitated, but not for long. It tried to drop through the opening in the landing, but it wouldn't fit. Instead, it leapt up so that for a second, all four of its feet balanced on the railing's edge. Then it leapt again, angling its feet toward the building, which it hit and bounced off, down onto the pavement, down the alley toward the street.

Now they were on the bottom landing, releasing the catch on the ladder. Will was still in front, leading like he was meant to lead a wild chase down eleven stories of a fire escape. He hopped onto the ladder, descended with it, and actually put his feet on the ladder rails like he was a firefighter.

"Right behind you, Will," shouted Kid.

The goat disappeared around the corner. Kid didn't stop to see how Bobby and Cat and the other man managed to get down, but by the time she'd turned the corner from the alley onto the street, they were right behind her.

Suddenly the tiny woman drew a deep, shuddering breath and leapt to her feet.

"I am sorry. I was wrong. I must go."

Jonathan looked quizzical. She ran past him, calling back over her shoulder, "My grandson, his parents died in the towers, he cannot look out windows, he cannot stand heights. And he is going on the roof! I should never have let him out of my sight."

Zip. Zip. Zip. A genius three-point turn. Jonathan was an expert now. Jonathan was cooking. He caught up to Dr. Lomp, poking the elevator button over and over.

"Oh, I can't wait. I'll take the stairs," said Dr. Lomp.

But the door opened just then. They got on. Dr. Lomp did to the P button what she'd done to the elevator call button. Poke. Poke. Poke. Poke. The doors closed. The elevator rose. Dinged. The doors opened.

The blind man stood there with his dog in harness in one hand and a laptop in his other, a giant grin on his face. Dr. Lomp practically ran into him.

"Pardon me." She moved right. He moved right. "I'll just — " She moved left. He moved left.

"Are you after the goat, too?" he said.

"The children, the children. Where are the children?" said Dr. Lomp. "Get out of my way."

"They're — "

But she didn't stay to hear his answer. Dr. Lomp ran out of the elevator, out the open door to the roof.

" — on the fire escape," finished the blind man.

Jonathan could see he thought he was now alone. He wanted to say something, to alert the man to his presence.

"O," he said.

"Augh," said the blind man, jumping.

"Ee," said Jonathan. He meant "sorry," but only the last syllable came out.

"Uh," said the blind man. "Sorry. You just surprised me. I didn't know anyone was there."

Dr. Lomp was back now. "They've gone down the fire escape. I am astonished. I would not have believed it. Come. We must catch up with them."

The elevator door began to close. The blind man threw out a hand to stop it. Dr. Lomp thanked him. Jonathan backed up to make room. Dr. Lomp and the man and his dog got on the elevator. Dr. Lomp poked L L L L.

The blind man was now looking bewildered. Jonathan tried to signal that he was unable to speak, but of course, the blind man could not see.

"I … 'an't 'peak," said Jonathan.

"I beg your pardon?"

Jonathan tried to get Dr. Lomp's attention to get her to explain, but she was too focused on the elevator.

"I. Can't. Sssspeak."

The blind man cocked his head. "I think you just did," he said.

"Ha," said Jonathan. Then they both had big grins on their faces.

They were almost at the lobby. The elevator dinged. The door opened. Dr. Lomp ran out, the blind man followed. Jonathan came last. Julio ran to hold the door. The goat sped past from left to right.

"What the …" said Julio.

Dr. Lomp ran through the door. The blind man ran through the door. He turned right, too, ran a few steps and then did something very strange.

He half dropped, half threw his laptop on the sidewalk and jumped on it. His feet caught just the edge of it and he fell on his rear end.

The goat chasers were almost upon him, so that when he fell, they tumbled over top of him — the two children, the man from the apartment, wearing only one shoe, and the skinny well-dressed man who was always talking about his hamsters.

Dr. Lomp, meantime, turned to run the other way, then cried out, "Will!" and fell on top of the blind man.

Only the two dogs escaped unscathed, dancing out of the way of the human pile-up.

Farther down the sidewalk, a thin, gawky, droopy-looking woman stood agape.

"Will," cried Dr. Lomp again.

"I'm fine, Bubcha," said the boy. "I did it. I came down the fire escape. I'm fine."

"Mom," cried the other kid.

"Kid?" said the droopy woman.

Julio let the door shut on Jonathan's scooter and stepped forward to help the others up from the pile, Dr. Lomp first.

"Yo. Joff," said Julio. "Did you think that was your skateboard? Man, where is your head at?"

"My head is in the clouds, Julio," said the blind man. "My head is in the clouds."

"See, Julio? There *is* a goat."

"The goat," said the other kid. "It's getting away."

They all turned to look. Cars honked. Traffic lurched as the drivers realized or failed to realize what was happening. The goat didn't run in front of cars or wait for them to stop. It leapt up on top of them and over them, from one to another to another to another. Up onto a hood, hood to roof, roof to next roof to next. And then in a neat flow it leapt to the cars coming the other way.

It was like the best circus act you'd ever seen. Between each car the goat seemed to give an extra little kick of its heels.

And then it was across.

They were all on their feet again, and running, and Jonathan went after them.

The goat had crossed against traffic. Now the Walk signal was lit, and the little crowd hotfooted across the street. But they were no match for the scooter. Jonathan hit the throttle. The little electric motor hummed higher and higher. He passed them. The goat was already well across the green toward the area where the forest began.

Somebody had to keep up. And that somebody was Jonathan.

But someone was in his way. Someone was on the path, still as a statue, arms hanging straight down as they do when people are dumbfounded.

Doris. He tore up to her, stopped in front. There was no way to let her know what was happening, but he gave her as much of a grin as he could manage. He tilted his head. Hop on. He made room on the foot platform for her. Doris hopped on.

"What ho, Jonathan," she shouted happily. "Lay on!"

•

The rest of them had caught up to Jonathan.

But the goat was losing them. It was heading into the undergrowth.

No, wait.

It was slowing down. It was lowering its head.

It was eating. Tearing up grass, tossing its head, chewing furiously, tearing up more.

The old man on the scooter tried to follow across the grass. The goat shied away, but not too far.

"Wait," called Kid, holding out her hands to stop the others.

"It's frightened," said Will.

They all stopped. The whole crowd of them. The old man, his wife, Will, Dr. Lomp, Kid, Lisa, Bobby, Cat, Joff, Michigan, the man with the hamsters.

"It doesn't need to be," said Kid. "But it is."

"It's young," said Dr. Lomp in wonder.

"No more than a — " Bobby flashed a grin. "Kid," he said.

"What do we do now?" said Lisa.

"We let it eat," said Kid.

They stood in silence, watching the goat eat.

Jonathan tapped Doris. He drew out the tablet and typed, *That's what's been eating your wheatgrass.*

Doris just hugged him and kissed his face. "Oh, Jonathan. You're back. Thank God."

"I walked on a roof," Will said. "I went over the edge of a roof. I went down a fire escape."

Dr. Lomp said, "You are free, Will. I am proud of you. Don't ever do that again."

"But, Bubcha — "

"No, I do not mean what I say. Do it again and again. Live your own life. Your parents are gone, we miss them, they died horribly, but you will not die the same way. In between now and then you will live. Your own life. With all my love." And she grasped him in a fierce hug.

A crowd gathered. Mrs. Grbzc was there.

"What does it look like?" asked Joff.

What did the goat look like? Young. Skinny. Ragged. Its coat was dingy and falling out in clumps.

But still. It looked like a wild animal. Just a block or so over, still in the very same park, you could see another mountain goat at the Central Park Zoo.

In some ways, seeing this one was no different.

In another way, it was completely different.

There was no enclosure. Nothing between them and it, with its new young horns, its wariness, its incredible agility.

"I will call the zoo," said the skinny man at last. He pulled out a cellphone, looked up the number and made the call. When he had explained where they were and that, yes, he really meant there was a mountain goat that had been living on their building and was now eating grass in Central Park, Kid could hear the person on the other end say, "How would a mountain goat get on your building?"

The man sighed. "It is a long story." He hung up. "I do not really have hamsters, I mean, guinea pigs," he said to the rest of them. "You see, my father loved to kayak and trek and backpack. I preferred the city." He told them a long and sad and beautiful story that ended with the goat — or his dad, he couldn't say which — leaping out the window.

There was a long silence.

Michigan meandered toward the goat. He lifted his leg on a bush. The goat kept eating. Michigan went closer, sniffed the goat's butt as if it were a dog. Moved a little away from it and rolled on his back. Got up again and bowed before the goat.

The goat understood. It hopped toward Michigan.

Michigan darted away. The goat planted its front legs and kicked its back legs.

The dog and the goat gamboled.

"It's like those unlikely-animal-friends videos on YouTube," said Bobby.

"Better," said Lisa.

A truck from the zoo came, with four excited zoo-keepers and a cage in the back. Two cops kept people away from the goat. One of the zookeepers had a rifle.

"Somebody get that dog out of the way."

"You're not going to shoot it," said Kid.

"It shoots tranquilizers," said the zookeeper.

"Do you have to?"

"A mountain goat will not walk into a cage," said Dr. Lomp.

"What she said," said the zookeeper.

Joff called Michigan. He immediately ran over.

Sometimes people said the city was wild. But a city was more than anything else a large collection of people. Smaller animals could work with that. Smaller animals could make a wilderness of small areas.

Big wild animals, no.

The zookeeper shot the dart.

The goat winced, looked up. Went back to eating. Fell to its knees. Turned its head. Keeled over.

Will gasped. Kid's hand flew to her heart. Will's hand flew to his mouth. Kid reached out with her free hand and took Will's free hand. It grasped hers.

A vet zookeeper listened to the goat's heart, gave a nod. The zookeepers loaded the limp goat into the cage and carried the cage back to the truck. They flipped up the tailgate and drove off.

"There really was a goat," said Lisa.

"I guess we're all going to have seven gears of lewd yuck," said Bobby.

"Can we handle that much?" said Lisa. Bobby hip-checked her.

Kid and Will let go their hands.

"Where's Cat?" said Kid.

She'd been sitting at Bobby's side not that long ago.

"Ca-at," called Kid.

"Ca-at," called Will.

"Catherine the Terrible," said Dr. Lomp.

Cat was making her way toward them through the crowd, now dispersing, a rat in her mouth.

"Drop it," said Dr. Lomp sternly. Cat dropped it.

"Your turn," said Bobby, fumbling in his pocket and coming up with a poo bag.

Lisa took the bag, put it on her hand, took a big breath and picked up the rat.

"We're picking up rats! In New York City!"

As Kid rolled her eyes, she caught glimpses of faces — friends and neighbors and strangers, traffic and trees and sky.

And over there, Doug's building. Goatless now, but a lot like home.

Thanks to Kate for laughing at the right bits, Jacqueline for asking every week if the book was done yet, and Cindy for unflagging support. To editor Shelley Tanaka, thanks for a sharp eye, deft hand and wise mind.

ANNE FLEMING is the author of *Pool-Hopping and Other Stories* (shortlisted for the Ethel Wilson Fiction Prize, the Danuta Gleed Award and the Governor General's Award), *Anomaly* and *Gay Dwarves of America*. She is a long-time and highly regarded teacher of creative writing who has taught at the University of British Columbia, Emily Carr University of Art and Design, Douglas College, Kwantlen University College and the Banff Centre for the Arts. *The Goat* is her first full-length work for young readers.

Anne lives in Vancouver.